PAY DIRT

   Suddenly Duke let out another bark, and Jed spun around. "You see something, Duke?"

   Duke pointed. Jed looked over to his right. There, feeding in the tall swamp grass, was that darn jackrabbit. Jed brought the shotgun to his shoulder, aimed, and squeezed the trigger.

   Boom! The shotgun fired. But even before the smoke cleared, Jed knew he'd missed the rabbit. All his buckshot had done was blast a hole in the soft earth at the edge of the swamp.

   "Dang it!" he shouted in frustration. "Granny's rabbit stew sure won't taste the same without no rabbit. Go git him, Duke!"

   Jed's trusty hound bounded off after the rabbit. Jed started to run after both of them.

   "Oooops!" Suddenly he slipped and landed flat on his back. He lay there for a moment, stunned. He looked over and noticed the hole in the ground his buckshot had made. Thick, black, gooey gunk was bubbling out of the hole.

   "Don't that beat all," he muttered.

   Then Jed heard a distant rumbling sound. Only it wasn't coming from anywhere *around* him. It was coming from *under* him. Now the ground beneath him began to tremble and shake.

   Jed staggered back from the shaking ground. No sooner had he stepped away than the hole suddenly burst open, and a huge geyser of jet-black, gooey liquid gushed high into the sky.

   "Look out, Duke!" Jed ~~threw up his~~ arm to protect his fa~~ce as the~~ black gunk poured d~~own,~~ covering them both.

Books by Todd Strasser

THE ACCIDENT
THE WAVE
BEYOND THE REEF
THE LIFEGUARDS
FRIENDS TILL THE END
THE FAMILY MAN
HOME ALONE

THE
BEVERLY
HILLBILLIES™

A novelization by
Todd Strasser

From the Motion Picture
THE BEVERLY HILLBILLIES
Screenplay by
Lawrence Konner & Mark Rosenthal
and Alex Herschlag & Rob Schneider
Story by
Lawrence Konner & Mark Rosenthal
Based upon the Television Series
created by Paul Henning

HarperPaperbacks
A Division of HarperCollinsPublishers

This is a work of fiction. The characters, incidents, and dialogues are products of the author's imagination and are not to be construed as real. Any resemblance to actual events or persons, living or dead, is entirely coincidental.

HarperPaperbacks   *A Division of* HarperCollins*Publishers*
10 East 53rd Street, New York, N.Y. 10022

Cover photograph courtesy of Twentieth Century Fox

First printing: November 1993

Printed in the United States of America

HarperPaperbacks and colophon are trademarks of HarperCollins*Publishers*

❖ 10 9 8 7 6 5 4 3 2 1

For Jessica and Rachel Brown

ONE

The red sun of dawn peeked over the green wooded hills of the Ozark Mountains. Fog lay in the valleys and mist hung over the still ponds and lakes. Birds chirped their morning songs and forest animals went about their lives, undisturbed by man or machine. For here, in the deepest part of the hills, civilization had barely made a dent. The few men and women who dwelled in the woods lived in harmony with nature and all its creatures, much the same way as people must have lived centuries ago. . . .

Up on a rocky ridge overlooking a valley sat a lanky, unshaven man. His name was Jed Clampett, and he wore a tattered wide-brimmed hat, a jacket made from animal skins, and a pair of old blue jeans. A thick, untrimmed mustache adorned his upper lip, and the skin of his face was weather-beaten and lined. But beneath the week-old stubble on his chin was the face of a kindly and simple man. Someone untouched by the supercharged world that surrounded his peaceful hills.

A long, old double-barrel shotgun lay on the dew-covered grass beside Jed. Nearby, an old chocolate-brown hound named Duke lay on his side with his eyes closed, dreaming of tasty raccoons.

With a sharp knife in his hand, Jed slowly whittled a piece of hickory. He heard a grumbling sound and knew it was his stomach. He shook his head and sighed. "Wouldn't mind findin' us some breakfast, Duke. Ain't much fun to sit here and whittle on an empty stomach."

The old hunting dog suddenly lifted his gray snout and sniffed the air as if he had understood him.

"Smell something, Duke?" Jed asked.

Duke got to his feet stiffly and pointed down

the hill. Jed squinted and saw something brown dart through the trees. It disappeared for a moment, then there it was again! A big old jackrabbit! Just the perfect thing for breakfast.

Grrrooofff! Duke barked, and took off down the hill.

"Stay with him, Duke!" Jed jumped up and grabbed his shotgun. "Maybe I'll get us some breakfast after all!"

Jed stumbled down the hill. Ahead, he watched the jackrabbit, with Duke hot on his tail, disappear into the dark forest below.

Either the rabbit was faster than Jed had expected, or he and Duke were getting slower with age. But pretty soon they lost sight of it. Jed found Duke sitting beneath a tall pine, panting for breath.

"Lost him, huh?" Jed asked in a disappointed tone as he gasped for breath himself. The sudden exercise made his stomach growl even louder for food. "Well, I guess now that I'm gettin' on toward fifty, I cain't run the way I used to. But come on, maybe we can track him awhile."

For the next hour Duke and Jed tracked the rabbit through the woods. Duke's legs might not have been able to carry him as fast as they once had, but his sense of smell was as sharp as ever. No matter how far ahead of them that rabbit got, Duke could still follow him.

And Jed followed Duke. Despite his hungry

3

stomach, there was nothing quite so nice as a brisk morning walk through the woods. Besides, the rabbit seemed to be leading Duke and him back around the lake toward the Clampett shack. So whether he bagged that rabbit or not, he'd soon be home.

By the side of a lake not far away, Jed's sixteen-year-old daughter, Elly May, knelt on the ground and stuffed moss into an old coffee can. The early-morning sunlight shimmered on her long blond hair, and her big blue eyes sparkled with girlish innocence. Her full lips were parted, revealing a bright, dazzling smile, and the tight T-shirt she wore was stretched to the limit by her voluptuous body.

Elly May lit the moss with a match, and smoke began to waft out of the can. Some of Elly May's friends—a possum, a squirrel, and a deer fawn—watched curiously. When the can had started smoking real good, Elly May kicked it into the opening at the base of a hollow tree stump nearby. Instantly a swarm of bees rose out of the stump to escape the smoke.

"Now, don't worry, fellers," Elly May told the bees as she dug her hand into the tree stump and removed a chunk of honeycomb dripping with golden honey. "I'll leave plenty for you. I just need a little for breakfast."

GRRROARRRR! A ferocious roar startled Elly May, and she instantly straightened up. In a flash, the critters she called friends raced away into the safety of the woods. Elly May spun around and found a huge grizzly bear rearing up on its hind legs behind her. Baring its six-inch razor-sharp claws, the bear took an angry swipe at the defenseless young girl.

Elly May barely managed to bat his paw away. The bear lunged forward, wrapping its huge furry arms around her and spilling honey all over her T-shirt.

As the bear began to squeeze her Elly May just managed to work her arms free. Then, in a quick, sudden move, she twisted around, dropped to one knee, and flipped the bear over her back.

Thud! The startled bear hit the ground hard. Before it could react, Elly May grabbed its hind leg and pinned it to the ground.

"I swear," she shouted angrily, "if you don't learn to start sharin' this honey, I'm gonna give you a real whompin'."

Elly May let go of the bear's leg and gave the huge creature the evil eye. The big furry beast whimpered, then turned and bolted back into the woods. Elly May looked down at her T-shirt. Thanks to that danged bear, it was all covered with honey. Now she'd have to jump in the lake and wash it off.

*   *   *

A little while later, as Duke and Jed pushed through the brush near the lakeshore, they stumbled into a clearing. Five of the local boys were sitting there, staring out at the lake. They were all wearing T-shirts and overalls, and all looked mighty surprised to see Jed there.

"Howdy, fellers," Jed said with a friendly wave. "Any of you boys see a jackrabbit scoot by here?"

The boys quickly scrambled to their feet, giving each other nervous looks out of the corners of their eyes and acting real jittery. Jed wondered what could be bothering them.

"Uh, we ain't seen nothin', Mr. Clampett," said the biggest among them, a huge, husky youth named Dwayne, who stood nearly six and a half feet tall and weighed close to three hundred pounds.

"What're you'all doin' down here so early anyway?" Jed asked, just being friendly.

"Just doin' a little fishin'," Dwayne replied. The other boys nodded eagerly.

Well, that made sense to Jed. The best time to go fishin' was early in the morning. But then he noticed something peculiar.

"Fishin' you say?"

"That's right, Mr. Clampett," Dwayne said. "This here's the best time of day to get yourself a mess of catfish."

"I reckon that to be true," Jed said. "But you boys ain't got no bait buckets."

Dwayne scowled and scratched his head as he looked around. "Well, now, you're right about that, Mr. Clampett."

"And you ain't got no lines neither," Jed pointed out.

"Right again, Mr. Clampett," Dwayne replied with a sheepish shrug.

"Why, you ain't even got no fishin' poles," Jed said. "Now, what kind of fishin' can you do without none of those things?"

Before Dwayne could answer, there was a splash a little ways out in the lake. Jed looked over and saw a head full of long, wet blond hair rise out of the water. Well, doggone! It was his daughter, Elly May!

Elly May stood up in the waist-deep water.

"Hey, Pa!" she called with a wave. "Me 'n my friends was just takin' a bath."

Jed saw an assortment of critters come up for air around her in the lake. There was a deer, a moose, a muskrat, and a beaver. It would have been a real quaint scene were it not for the fact that Elly May's skimpy T-shirt clung to her voluptuous body in a most revealing away.

Jed glanced at Dwayne and his friends and gave them a cold look. "Fishin' you said?"

" 'Scuse me, sir." Dwayne swallowed hard and

started to back away. "I heard them new Elvis stamps is in at the post office."

"You did, huh?" Jed said with a slight smirk.

"Uh, yes, sir," Dwayne said. "Me an' the boys, we were just thinkin' of becoming stamp collectors. Wasn't we, boys?"

The other boys nodded.

"Sure."

"Always wanted to collect stamps."

"Figured I might become one of those philatelic kind of fellers."

They were all backing away slowly, their eyes glued to the long barrels of Jed's shotgun.

"Well, that seems to me like a right honest and healthy hobby for a bunch of boys your age," Jed said approvingly. "A lot better'n going fishin' early in the morning with no fishin' poles."

"You're right about that, Mr. Clampett," Dwayne said, casting one last quick glance at Elly May. "See you around."

"Sure thing, boys." Jed watched as Dwayne hurried away followed by the rest of the boys. When they'd all gone, he turned and looked again at Elly May, who was walking out of the lake toward him. Being Elly May's kin, Jed worked hard to keep his gaze above the level of her neck. But he had to admit to himself that there were certain aspects of his daughter that had changed greatly over the past few years. As a

protective father, he felt it was his duty to warn her about certain things that came with becoming a young lady.

"Now, Elly May," he said. "What do you think you're doin', swimmin' around out there in barely nothing more than your birthday suit?"

Elly May, the picture of youthful innocence, looked down at herself as if she were surprised. "Why, I didn't mean no harm."

"Of course you didn't," Jed said. "But did you see them fellers? They was watchin' you like cats 'neath a sparrow's nest."

"You mean Dwayne and those boys?" Elly May asked.

"Why, I most certainly do."

"But, Pa, those boys and me been swimmin' together ever since we was all pups," Elly May tried to explain. "They seen it all before."

"Well, them pups done grown into a pack of dogs," Jed warned her. "Now, you run on home and put on some dry clothes that don't show off so much of your . . . er . . . personality."

"Well, okay, Pa." Elly May shrugged. Then she shook her head back and forth like some dog that had just gotten out of a bath. Jed and Duke got sprayed with water. Elly May laughed and ran off into the woods, accompanied by all those critters that seemed to just follow her wherever she went.

But at least those animals were *real* animals. . . .

Suddenly Duke let out another bark, and Jed spun around. "You see something, Duke?"

Duke pointed. Jed looked over to his right, where the lake met up with an old swamp filled with cattails and mossy trees. There, feeding in the tall swamp grass, was that darn jackrabbit. Jed quickly brought the shotgun to his shoulder, aimed, and squeezed the trigger.

Boom! The shotgun fired, and the kick knocked Jed backward a few feet. But even before the smoke cleared, he knew he'd missed the rabbit. All his buckshot had done was blast a hole in the soft earth at the edge of the swamp.

"Dang it!" Jed shouted in frustration. "Granny's rabbit stew sure won't taste the same without no rabbit. Go git him, Duke!"

Jed's trusty hound bounded off after the rabbit, which had hightailed it straight into the swamp. Once again Jed started to run after both of them.

"Oooops!" Suddenly he slipped and landed flat on his back. He lay there for a moment, staring up at the blue sky, stunned. He looked over and noticed the hole in the ground he'd made when he'd missed that jackrabbit. Thick, black, gooey gunk was bubbling out of the hole.

"Don't that beat all," he muttered. He had never seen anything like it.

Then Jed heard a distant rumbling sound. Only it wasn't coming from anywhere *around*

him. It was coming from *under* him. Now the ground beneath him began to tremble and shake.

Sensing his master was in danger, Duke gave up chasing the rabbit and came barreling back. He stood nearby and barked excitedly.

"I know what you mean," Jed muttered as he started to get up. "I don't know what's goin' on, but I'm feeling as anxious as a long-tailed cat in a roomful of rockin' chairs."

Jed staggered back from the shaking ground. No sooner had he stepped away than the hole suddenly burst open, and a huge geyser of jet-black, gooey liquid gushed high into the sky.

"Look out, Duke!" Jed shouted, lifting his arm to protect his face. But it was too late. The black gunk poured down on him and his dog, covering them both.

"Darn," he muttered. "Now I done ruined a perfectly good swamp."

Jed turned and hurried away before any more of the stuff could get on him. As it was, Granny was gonna have a fit and a half when she saw his clothes.

"Come on, Duke," he called to the hound. "Let's get on home. I done lost my appetite for breakfast anyway."

TWO

The Clampett cabin was a one-room shack with wood shingles, a rough wooden door, a couple of small windows, and a porch. An old rain barrel stood beside the house to collect rainwater, and a lumpy stone chimney rose out of the roof. Underfed chickens pecked through the dirt around the house, and a couple of scrawny goats poked through the garbage, looking for anything even remotely edible.

Surrounding the shack were several smaller sheds. These included a chicken coop, a smoke shed for smoking meat and fish, and an outhouse with a crescent moon cut high into the door.

Out behind the house, Granny Clampett was tending her still. Granny was a spry old woman. Her gray hair was combed tightly against her head and pulled back into a bun. Above it she wore a small ruffled hat. The rest of her outfit consisted of an old, worn dress, an apron, a thin sweater that she wore even on the hottest of days, long underwear, and heavy boots.

She also wore thin, wire-rim eyeglasses—not that she'd ever been to the eye doctor, or even knew that eye doctors existed. But one day, years back, a government revenuer had come snooping around, and Granny had taken a shot at him with her shotgun. Unfortunately her eyes had gotten so bad that she missed. But she did manage to scare the feller so bad that he dropped his glasses and ran off. Granny picked up the glasses and tried them on. They improved her sight dramatically. She decided to wear them, and from then on she rarely missed her targets.

Granny bent down and blew on the fire under the still. The still was a simple affair, just a large, closed copper kettle cooking over a fire. From the top of the kettle a long curling tube of copper led to a glass mason jar. As drops of clear sour-mash moonshine dripped from the end of the copper tubing into the mason jar, Granny and several anxious "patients" watched closely. Among them was Miss Williams, an old spinster neighbor lady; Reverend Mason, an old wrinkle-faced Bible thumper whose bad back had him completely bent over; and Fat Elmer, a portly, red-faced farmer.

"Well, I reckon that's plenty," Miss Williams said, eager to get her hands on the jar.

"No, it ain't," Granny corrected her. "If you want to buy my medicine, you got to take the jar full."

"But I'm gettin' tired of waitin'," Miss Williams complained as the clear drops slowly fell into the jar.

"Cain't say I know why," Granny replied. "Seems like you've already been here twice this week."

"I know I've been here twice," said Miss Williams. "But my lumbago got me writhin' like a hoochie-coochie gal." As if to emphasize her point, she pressed her hand into the small of her back and bent backward with a loud groan.

Taking pity on her, Granny pulled away the almost full mason jar and replaced it with an empty one. Miss Williams quickly handed her a couple of wrinkled dollar bills and took the jar.

"You know, prevention is the latest thing with us doctors," Granny told her. "I'm prescribing two sips as needed until relief comes. Uh, you can start anytime."

Miss Williams lifted the jar to her lips and took a big gulp. When she brought the jar down again, she had a big smile on her face.

"Why, Granny, my arthritis done vanished totally," she exclaimed.

"Thought you said it was your lumbago," Granny said.

"That's right," said Miss Williams. "I'm feelin' so good, they both done gone away!"

"Well, come on back whenever you want," Granny said. "The doctor is always in."

Miss Williams went off, taking a slightly crooked path through the woods. Now Reverend Mason stumbled up, all bent over and running his gnarled fingers through his thinning white hair.

"You got a bad case of old-timer's disease, Reverend Mason," Granny told him. "This'll cure it."

She handed him a jar, and the reverend took a big gulp of moonshine. Still bent over, he slowly set the jar down. For a moment it looked like Granny's "medicine" wasn't going to help after all.

Suddenly Reverend Mason did a back flip and landed on his feet standing straight as a flagpole.

"Jumpin' Jehoshaphat!" he cried. "Makes me feel seventy again."

Granny smiled proudly. "Now, Reverend, if anyone in your parish is ailin', send 'em over for some of Dr. Daisy's Death Defier."

"I most certainly will," the reverend said. Then he clicked his heels and set off.

Fat Elmer, the rotund farmer, was next in line.

"Now, what ails you, Fat Elmer?" Granny asked.

"I done ate too much cheese," Elmer complained. "Now I cain't burp."

Granny fixed him up some moonshine, and in no time Fat Elmer was burpin' up a storm. He paid her and went off. Granny smiled to herself and threw another piece of wood onto the fire under the still. It was a good business, helpin' people the way she did. Maybe she ought to have a taste of that "medicine" herself, she thought. Just to make sure it was the right strength. She took an old, dented flask out of her dress and filled it, then took a good long drink.

Why, it tasted just fine! Granny put the mason jar down and did a little jig. There was nothin' like some good "medicine" to make a gal feel young again.

Not far away Jed and Duke trudged up the trail through the woods, toward the shack. Both man and dog were still covered with black goo.

Ahead, Jed saw Reverend Mason strolling toward him with a big smile on his face.

"'Mornin', Reverend." Jed tipped his hat.

"Howdy, Jed," the reverend replied. "Lose a hog in the mud?"

"Naw, I got me a big mess down in the swamp," Jed said with a sigh. "It's afloatin' in tar. I sure could use some help cleanin' it up."

"In times of trouble, I always look to the Good Book for help," Reverend Mason replied, opening his Bible. "Here it is. 'Cleanliness is next to godliness. No job too big or too small.'"

"The Bible says that?" Jed asked.

"Yup, and so do the Scagg Brothers." Reverend Mason handed Jed a small, white business card. "Their prices are negotiable. If you'd like, I'll send 'em along."

"I'd be much obliged," Jed replied. After all, he couldn't just leave the swamp like that.

He and Duke continued up the path toward the shack. Ahead they could see Granny dancing around like she was at a hootenanny or something.

"Now what're you dancin' around like that fer?" Jed asked.

Granny spun around and stared at Jed and Duke. Both man and dog were covered from head to foot with some kind of oily black slime.

"Why, Jedediah Clampett, what in the world happened to you?" Granny asked.

Jed sat down hard on a stump and tried to pull his boots off. But his hands kept slipping on the black slime.

"I knew I shoulda sold that swamp back when old man Jenkins wanted it last year," he muttered angrily at himself.

"Is it overrun with copperheads?" Granny asked.

"Nope." Jed shook his head.

"Filled with quicksand?"

"Not that neither," said Jed. "It's worse. Darn swamp's afloatin' with tar. Why, that sticky goop's everywhere!"

"Maybe you could get old man Jenkins to reconsider his offer," Granny suggested slyly. "Just don't tell him nothin' about the tar."

"Cain't," Jed said. "My conscience wouldn't allow it. I ain't gonna unload a ruined piece of property just to make a dollar."

"Well, you'll think of somethin'," Granny said. But she could see that he was feelin' pretty gloomy. If only there was something she could do. Suddenly she thought of it.

"Ya hungry, Jed?" she asked. "I got some possum innards and squirrel's feet left over from last night."

"You do?" A smile creased Jed's oil-streaked face.

"Yup."

"Well, doggone, that's good news," Jed said, getting up. "Them possum innards always taste better the second day."

Jed followed Granny up to the shack. He stopped beside the rain barrel and got washed up

as best he could. By the time he got to the door, Granny had the possum innards on the wood stove and was heating them up. In the meantime she'd taken out her sewing and was mending a few things.

Jed stepped into the shack. The decorations were few and simple. A handmade table and three chairs—for Granny, Elly May, and himself— a few shelves with cooking utensils, some kerosene lanterns, and a small porcelain sink with a hand pump that brought cold fresh water from an underground spring beneath the house.

"Jed," Granny said as he entered the shack. "You got to do something about that youngern of yours."

"Why?" Jed asked. "She get into trouble?"

"Yesterday I caught her rasslin' with that bobcat again." Granny held up a leather vest that was ripped straight down the middle. "Look what she done."

"Get hurt?" Jed asked.

"I reckon so," Granny said. "The old cat went limpin' off on three legs."

"I swear I don't know what I'm gonna do about that girl," Jed said wearily, recalling the scene he'd stumbled upon down by the lake that morning.

"Well, the first thing to do is get her into a dress," Granny said. "She's gettin' too big to be wearin' man's duds."

Granny reached down and picked up a shirt. "Looky here. She done popped the buttons off her shirt again."

"Well, Elly May carries herself proud," Jed tried to explain. "With her shoulders throwed back."

Granny looked at him over the tops of her glasses. "Believe me, Jed, it ain't her shoulders that's been poppin' these buttons."

Jed winced a little, but he knew Granny was right. Elly May was developing in ways he'd never thought a daughter of his would. If only her ma was still alive. She'd know how to handle her.

Jed went over to the sink and pumped himself some water to wash his hands. The rainwater outside hadn't been much use in getting the tar off, so he figured he might try some of the lye soap Granny sometimes made out of wood ashes.

"Elly May's a fully growed-up, rounded-out female woman and it's time she started acting like one," Granny said.

"Well, one of these days some boy'll come along and start courtin' her," Jed said, working up a lather in the sink. "Then she'll get the idea."

"I don't know about that," Granny said. "They came courtin' when she was twelve. And what'd she do?"

The memory brought a smile to Jed's face. "She whomped the tar out of 'em."

"Well, it ain't fittin'," Granny said. "Girl runnin' around as wild as a cougar, rasslin', fightin', and huntin'. She ought to be doin' woman's work."

"Like what?" Jed asked.

"She could start by helpin' me with the still," Granny said.

"Well, I'll speak to her," Jed said, although the truth was that he was uncomfortable about such things and generally forgot to do them.

Granny served up the possum innards and they tasted right fine. Afterward Jed's stomach wasn't growling anymore, and he felt pretty contented. A full day spread out before him and there was plenty to do. That hole in the chicken coop needed mending, and a leak in the roof needed patching. The firewood was running low and needed to be replenished, and it was about time to plant some more corn.

Faced with all that, Jed went out back and found a good piece of hickory to whittle.

THREE

About a week later Jed was walking along with Duke down by the swamp when he heard the sounds of engines roaring and men shouting. What the devil could be goin' on? he wondered. Sort of curious, he snuck through the brush and brambles and hunkered down behind a rock, where he couldn't be seen.

But what he saw amazed him. Down in the

swamp, that gooey black tar was now spurting up out of three holes, not one. Not only that, but there were all sorts of fellers running around wearing yellow hard hats and long yellow coats streaked with the black stuff. Some of them were riding on big yellow machines, the likes of which Jed had never seen before. These machines had big shovels in front of them, and were so big and strong that they could actually dig huge gaping holes in the ground.

It must have been them Scagg boys the Reverend Mason had recommended. Jed figured they were probably trying to gauge how big a job it was going to be before they quoted him a price.

Then Jed saw something that really got him worried. Standing off near the shore, watching all this activity, were a couple of policemen in blue uniforms. Uh-oh, he thought. It looked like trouble. Maybe it was time to head back up to the shack and talk to Granny about it.

A little while later he was just coming up to the shack when he noticed a commotion out by the still. That little razorback piglet of Granny's was chasing the goats around, squealing up a storm. Then Jed saw what the problem was. The pig had gotten its snout into a jar of Granny's hooch and drunk a bunch of it. Jed grabbed the little pig and took him into the house.

"Granny," he called, pushing the backdoor

open. "This little pig of yours got into the still again."

Granny looked up from her sewing. "He drink much?"

"I reckon he did," Jed said. "He was chasin' the goats all over the yard, and they're about ten times his size."

Granny took the pig. "That's the trouble with razorbacks. They make such mean drunks. I'll put him back in the pen."

Granny went out the backdoor. Now there was a bunch of banging from the front door. "Pa? Granny?" Elly May shouted from outside. "Somebody open the door."

Jed went over and pulled open the door. Elly May was standing outside, carrying a man over her shoulder. Jed recognized him as one of them yellow-jacketed fellers he'd just seen down by the swamp.

"Howdy, Pa!" Elly May exclaimed cheerfully as she brushed past him and laid the feller out on the kitchen table. Poor feller appeared to be unconscious.

"What you got there, Elly May?" Jed asked.

"A stranger," Elly May replied.

"How'd you get him?" Jed asked.

"I beaned him with a rock," Elly May said proudly.

"What fer?" Jed asked.

"He was sneakin' around down by the lake,"

Elly May explained. "I thought he might be a revenuer tryin' to track down Granny's still."

"Well, he ain't no revenuer," Jed said.

Elly May brightened considerably. "Then, can I keep him?"

"Of course not," Jed replied.

"Why not?" Elly May asked with a frown. "I caught him."

"That don't matter."

"Well, he won't be no trouble," Elly May said. "I can keep him out in the smokehouse."

"Elly May, you cain't keep people like they're dogs and cats," Jed tried to explain.

Granny came in from the back. "Who's that?" she asked when she saw the body on the kitchen table.

"Some feller Elly May found snoopin' around down by the lake," Jed said.

"I beaned him with a rock so he'd be easier to tote," Elly May explained.

Granny took a good hard look at him. "That there feller's from the petroleum company."

"What's a petroleum?" Jed asked. He'd never heard of such a thing.

"Don't know," Granny said. "He came to the door this morning and asked if he could do some wildcattin' down by the lake. I said help yerself. We's glad to get rid of the critters."

"What'd he say?" Jed asked.

"He just laughed," Granny said. "But the

joke's on him. There ain't been no wildcats around here for thirty years."

The man on the table groaned and pushed himself up onto his elbows. He stared up at the Clampetts with bleary eyes and rubbed the bump on his head. "Where am I?" he asked groggily.

"This here's the Clampett place," Jed answered. "My name's Jed Clampett. This here's my youngern, Elly May. And that's Granny. Granny says you've been doin' some wildcattin'."

"Uh, there's no need to," the man said. "Listen, Mr. Clampett, you wouldn't happen to know who owns the land around here, would you?"

"Why, it all belongs to—" Elly May started to reply, but Jed quickly shushed her. The memory of the police around the swamp that morning was still fresh in his mind. He stuck his thumbs under his suspenders and eyed the stranger suspiciously.

"Why do you want to know?" he asked.

"Well, that swamp is full of oil," the stranger said.

"Looked like tar to me," Jed said.

"Tar, oil, it's all the same thing," the man said. "My company would like to pump it out."

Then he was right, Jed thought. This must've been one of them Scagg boys.

"Well, I'd like that, too," he said, recalling all the heavy machinery. "But I'm not sure I can afford to have it done right now."

"Then it's your land?" the man asked with wide eyes.

Jed nodded regretfully.

"Well, you don't understand," the man said. "You wouldn't have to pay for us to pump the oil out."

Jed eyed him even more suspiciously. "Well, I don't usually take favors from strangers."

The man gasped. "No, no. You don't understand, Mr. Clampett. You're a very rich man."

The feller was talking pure nonsense. Jed glanced over at Elly May. "How big a rock did you say you beaned this feller with?"

"No bigger than a hedge apple," Elly May said.

"Listen," the man from the petroleum company said, getting off the kitchen table and looking around, "I've got to call my office in Tulsa. Have you got a telephone?"

"A what?" Jed squinted at him. The feller was making less and less sense every moment.

"A telephone," the man said in a tone that implied that it was something everyone had. Jed glanced back at Granny and Elly May and rolled his eyes.

"Maybe one of your neighbors has one," the man said.

"Well, I wouldn't know," Jed said, playing along. "Maybe you ought to try describing it to me."

"Well, out here in the sticks it's probably a black plastic thing about the size of a small loaf of bread," the man said.

"Plastic?" Jed asked. "What's that."

"You don't know what plastic is?" the man asked, amazed. "Why, it's the substance that practically everything is made out of these days."

"We got any around here?" Granny asked.

The man looked around the room and frowned. "Actually you don't. Uh, but you know all that oil down in your swamp? That's what plastic is made of."

"But that stuff's all gooey and liquidlike," Elly May said.

"That's right," said the man. "But scientists can turn it into hard plastic. And then it gets turned into all kinds of things. Like telephones and car parts and computers."

Jed wasn't even going to bother asking what a computer was. He just put his hand on the petroleum man's shoulder and started to lead him back to the kitchen table.

"What are you doing?" the man asked.

"I think you better lie down some more," Jed said. "You gotta relax and sort things out."

"No, believe me," the man said, backing away. "Everybody has telephones. And if you had one, I'd punch in my credit card number, call my company in Tulsa, and tell my boss I was standing in the house of one of the richest men in the country."

Jed glanced back at Granny and Elly May. Granny shook her head and Elly May looked sad. Jed guessed she probably wouldn't want to keep this feller now even if they let her.

"Okay, look, forget it," the man from the petroleum company said. "I'll fly back to Tulsa and tell my boss in person."

"Fly?" Jed asked, surprised.

"Look, don't try to figure it out," the man said. "Just promise me that you won't sell that swamp to anyone until you get our offer. Will you promise me?"

Jed didn't see what harm it would do to promise the feller that. After all, no one in their right mind would buy that swamp now that it was all full of oil. And besides, when you made a promise to someone who thought they could fly, it wasn't like you really had to keep it.

"Sure, I'll promise you that," Jed said. He extended his hand, and the man from the petroleum company shook it.

"Now, you keep that promise," the man said. "And don't be surprised if my boss flies in here personally tomorrow to make the deal."

"No, I won't be at all surprised," Jed said with a smile.

"Great. Thanks!" The man dashed out the door.

Jed closed the door and looked back at Granny and Elly May. "You hear that? He says his boss is gonna fly in here personally tomorrow."

"Well, you didn't check under that yellow coat," Granny said with a grin. "Maybe he's got wings."

"Yup," Jed said with a smile. "Maybe them folks up in Tulsa *all* got wings these days."

FOUR

The next afternoon Jed was sitting at the kitchen table, picking on his banjo. Elly May sat beside him, feeding a small goat from a baby bottle. Suddenly it started to sound awful windy outside. The front door flew open and Granny raced in, looking very excited.

"It's a twister, Jed!" she cried frantically. "Bar the windows! Git the chickens to the coop! I'm goin' out back to save the still!"

A twister? Jed frowned. Wasn't the right time of year for a twister. Not only that, but he'd been outside just minutes before and the weather was clear and warm.

Jed stepped outside. Granny was right about one thing. It sure was windy, and that wind was making one heck of a racket. The clothes were getting blown off the clothesline, the flowerpots were crashing down from the window ledges. Duke was barking up a storm.

Elly May came running up. "What is it, Pa? What's goin' on?"

"Cain't say fer sure, Elly May," Jed shouted over the noise of the wind. "Some kind of freak storm, I guess."

Meanwhile Granny was running around like a chicken with its head cut off.

"We better grab her before she hurts herself!" Jed shouted. He and Elly May raced after Granny and finally snatched her up by her arms and legs.

"Take her into the house!" Jed shouted.

By now Granny was convinced that the end had come.

"It's the big wind comin' to carry me away to the final judgment," she moaned. "Oh Lord, I swear I only made moonshine for medicinal purposes. I never enjoyed it as it went down! Not one swallow!"

They'd just got Granny into the shack when some strange kind of flying contraption landed in

the front yard, kicking up dust, loose twigs, and leaves, like a regular dust storm. The contraption looked like some kind of giant mechanical insect. Jed watched in amazement from the window of the shack as two men in dark suits climbed out.

"What is it, Pa?" Elly May gasped.

"Don't reckon I know," Jed replied. "Cain't say I've ever seen anything quite like it before."

"Well, who do you think those men are?" Elly May asked.

"Well, I hate to say it, but they look a whole lot more like revenuers than that yellow-jacketed feller that was here yesterday."

"Revenuers!" Granny gasped. "They come to take me away in that darn contraption of theirs! That's just as bad as the Lord takin' me away on Judgment Day!"

"Now, hold on tight, Granny," Jed reassured her. "No one's takin' anyone anywhere."

The men in dark suits arrived at the front door and knocked. Elly May and Granny gave Jed worried looks, but Jed just brought his finger to his lips and gestured for them to be silent.

Once again the men outside knocked. "Jed Clampett?" one of them called. "Mr. Clampett, are you in there?"

Jed didn't utter a peep. He was hoping that they'd think no one was home, and just leave. But the men outside banged on the door again.

"Mr. Clampett," one of them said. "We have

some good news that will be most beneficial to you. Please let us in."

Elly May and Granny gave Jed looks, but Jed shook his head and stood firm. That talk about good news was just an old revenuers' trick to get him to open the door.

The men outside banged again. "Mr. Clampett, please! We saw you go into the house just before we landed."

Hmmm. That was a tough one, but Jed thought he had a solution.

"How do you folks know I ain't got some secret tunnel out of my house and into the woods?" he asked through the door.

His question was met with silence. Then one of the men said, "Well, we don't know if you do or not, sir."

Elly May and Granny nodded approvingly. Jed smiled at them and turned back to the door. "Well, then how do you know I'm still in my house? How do you know I ain't snuck down my secret tunnel out into the woods?"

"Well, sir," one of the men said. "If you'd done that, you wouldn't be speaking to us right now, would you?"

Jed rubbed his chin. The feller outside had a good point. Jed glanced back at Elly May and Granny. "What should we do?" he whispered.

"Shoot 'em?" Granny asked, picking up Jed's big double-barrel shotgun.

Jed shook his head. "It ain't right to do that, Granny. They ain't done nothin' bad to us."

"Not *yet* they ain't," Granny snapped.

Jed turned back to the door. "Listen here, fellers. If I let you in, will you promise not to take Granny away? She's gettin' a little too old to go to jail."

"Mr. Clampett, sir," one of the men said. "We have no reason to put her in jail. We're not the police. We're from the petroleum company."

"Like that stranger I found," Elly said.

"Was one of your boys around here yesterday?" Jed asked through the door. "Sort of confused fellow wearing a yellow coat? Talked a lot of nonsense about being able to fly."

"Well, I don't know about the confused part," the man on the other side of the door said. "But yes, that fellow works for our company."

Jed turned back to Granny and Elly May. "Remember the feller yesterday said how he wanted to clean up the swamp? Well, Reverend Mason said he was gonna send some fellers called the Scagg brothers over to talk about doin' just that. I didn't think of it before, but maybe that feller who was here yesterday works for 'em."

"I still think they're revenuers in disguise," Granny said.

Jed turned back to the door. "You boys swear you're not revenuers in disguise?"

"You have my word, Mr. Clampett."

Jed sighed and turned to Granny. "He gave his word, Granny. I don't think we can run away from this thing."

"I know it, but I still don't trust 'em," Granny replied.

"Well, around here a man's word is all he's got," Jed said.

"I reckon," Granny agreed sadly. "All right, let 'em in."

Jed went to the front door and pulled it open. The men looked around and stepped cautiously into the shack. Both of them were carrying flat leather boxes with handles.

"Are you Mr. Clampett?" The man who asked this was portly and balding, with a red face. It was obvious to Jed that he didn't get enough exercise.

"I am, sir," Jed replied.

"My name's Briggs," the portly man said, shaking Jed's hand. "And this is my associate, Danforth."

Danforth was younger and trimmer looking than Briggs. He had short, curly blond hair. Briggs had called him an "associate," but Jed knew a high-pressure salesman when he saw one.

"I'm told you are the rightful owner of this land," Briggs said to Jed. "Is that correct?"

Jed nodded quietly, dreading what was coming. "Reverend Mason must've sent you fellers, right?"

The two men glanced at each other. "Uh, sure, that's right, the Reverend Mason sent us," the one named Danforth said.

"Can you tell me how you came to be the owner?" Briggs asked.

Jed looked over at Granny. As she was the oldest living member of the Clampett clan, he left most historical matters to her.

"Well, sonny," Granny said. "His great-great-grandpa bought this land from the Ouachita tribe way back before this state was even called Arkansas. Every inch of it is his."

Briggs glanced back at Danforth, who nodded. "That is what our research department reported, too, sir."

"Well, let's not beat around the bush, gentlemen," Jed said. "Before I sign anything, I kinda like to know how much money we're talkin' about."

The men glanced at each other and seemed reluctant to speak. Jed thought he knew why. "Granny, Elly May, you get on with your chores and leave us menfolk to discuss this matter."

Granny went over to the stove and started to stir a pot. Elly May picked up a lamb and started to feed it with a baby's bottle. Jed turned back to Briggs and Danforth.

"All right, gentlemen," he said. "Fire away."

"Well, I assume you understand why we're here, Mr. Clampett," Briggs said. "This kind of thing only happens once in a lifetime."

Jed winced a little. He didn't think it was *that* bad.

"We're talking about a lot of money, Mr. Clampett," Danforth said. "I assure you, we're all going to clean up on this deal."

"Why should I clean up?" Jed asked, perplexed.

"Because there is more petroleum in your swamp than there is in all of Kuwait," Briggs said.

"You can forget Prudhoe Bay, Mr. Clampett," Danforth said. "Forget Kuwait. Forget the North Sea. This is bigger. Much bigger."

Jed rubbed his hand over his face. "That much, huh? Cain't you just toss it in some barrels and truck it out?"

"No, sir," said Briggs. "With something this big, we'll need to run it down a pipeline to the coast."

Jed shook his head sadly. He felt Granny touch his shoulder sympathetically. He could see that he wasn't going to get out of this easily. It was time to face the music. "Elly May," he said. "Go get the jar."

"But, Pa, that's our rainy-day security money," Elly May said.

Jed heard her, but he knew she didn't understand the seriousness of the situation. These men wouldn't come all the way out there in that fancy flying contraption unless the situation was very, very grave.

"Do as I said, Elly May."

"We've weathered worse than this, Jed," Granny said grimly. "We'll be okay."

Elly May brought over a brown clay jug. Jed reached over to the corner and picked up a small ax. Briggs and Danforth quickly stepped back, but Jed meant them no harm. He swung the ax and smashed the jug. A large pile of coins and some crumpled dollars spilled out onto the table.

"Well, there it is," he said with a heavy sigh. "My life's savings. I figure you got about two hundred here. You can take it, Briggs. It's all I have. You got my word."

Jed pushed the money toward them. Briggs and Danforth gave each other puzzled looks.

"I don't think you understand, Mr. Clampett," Briggs said.

"Oh, I understand pretty well," Jed replied. "My swamp done sprung a petroleum leak and now we have to pay for it."

"On the contrary, Mr. Clampett," said Briggs. "We're going to pay *you*."

"Watch out, Jed," Granny warned. "It's a trick!"

"Now, let me get this straight," Jed said. "Are you fellers sayin' you want to pay *me* to clean the tar out of my own swamp?"

"Tar?" Briggs smiled. "Mr. Clampett, that tar is pure bitumen, benzene . . . *petroleum*. Your land is awash with oil."

"Well, call it what you will," Jed said with a shrug.

"Sir," said Danforth. "Oil is a valuable commodity. We are here to make you a very serious offer. We want to buy your oil."

Jed was totally confused. "Hold on now. Ain't you Briggs Scagg and Danforth Scagg, the Scagg brothers?"

"No, we're from Ozark Mountain Oil," Briggs said. "Mr. Clampett, you're sitting on the biggest domestic oil strike in history. As I said, we want to pay you for your oil."

"Just how much are you fellers talkin' about?" Granny asked.

"Well, before we make our offer," Briggs said, "let me remind you that we are all the victims of government regulations. It's become hard for oil companies to eke out a living these days."

"All right," Jed said. "We understand that."

Briggs motioned to Danforth, who flipped out a small device with numbered buttons on it. Jed watched as the feller quickly pushed a whole bunch of buttons. All sorts of numbers flashed up on a little screen above the buttons.

"Mind if I ask what that thing is?" Jed asked.

"This?" Danforth looked surprised. "It's a pocket calculator."

"What's it do?" Granny asked.

"Well, it adds and subtracts and multiplies and divides," Danforth explained.

"Oh, I know what that is," Elly May said.

"Cousin Jethro told me he learned how to do some of that in school."

"Ain't you been to school, mister?" Granny asked.

"Why, yes," Danforth said. "In fact, I have a master's degree in finance."

"Well, if you got all that highfalutin stuff, how come you need that little machine to help you add and subtract?" Granny asked.

"Well, I only use this for very complex equations," Danforth explained. "For instance, before I can estimate what we should pay you, I have to take into account land depreciation over twenty years, then add energy credits, minus windfall profit, five-point state surcharge, exploration tax, EPA regulations, landscape restoration, county permits, capital gains. . . ."

Danforth went on and on, his fingers racing over the calculator's keyboard. Jed knew he was just trying to prepare them for the paltry offer they were about to make for the swamp.

"Well, what's left for us folks?" Granny asked.

"Hmmm . . ." Danforth frowned and pushed a few more buttons. "That's eight, no, nine . . . Oh, what the hell, in round numbers let's just say it's one billion dollars."

"A billion?" Jed frowned.

"Is there something wrong with that?" Briggs asked nervously.

"Well, I've heard of gold dollars," Jed said. "I've heard of silver dollars and paper dollars, but I ain't never heard of no billion dollars. I guess you're gonna tell me now that it's some new kind of dollar, right?"

Briggs and Danforth looked flabbergasted.

"Uh, Mr. Clampett," Danforth said quickly, picking up one of the crumpled dollar bills lying on the table. "Let me try to explain. You see this dollar?"

"Sure I do," Jed said.

"Well, I want you to imagine ten of them."

"All right." Jed could do that.

"Now, if you had ten piles of ten, how much would that be?" Danforth asked.

"Why it'd be a hundred," Jed said. "Any fool knows that."

"Now, suppose you had ten piles, and each pile had a hundred in it," Danforth said. "How much would that be?"

Jed glanced nervously at Granny. But she just shrugged.

"It would be a thousand dollars," Danforth said. "Now, Mr. Clampett, does a thousand dollars seem like a lot of money to you?"

"Well, if it's the same as ten piles of one hundred, then it sure is," Jed said. "In fact, it's probably more money than's run through my hands in my entire life."

"I thought so," Danforth said. "Now I want

you to try to imagine the following, Mr. Clampett. I want you to imagine a *thousand* piles, and each pile is a thousand dollars. Now, does *that* seem like a lot of money?"

"Well, it sure does," Jed said. "That's probably more money than there is in all of these here United States."

"Not quite," Mr. Briggs said with a smile.

"So are you tellin' us that a billion dollars is a thousand piles, and each pile is a thousand dollars?" Granny asked.

"No," Danforth said. "That's only a *million* dollars. Now, if you were to take that million dollars and make a thousand piles just like it, *then* you'd have a billion dollars."

Silence descended over the shack. Jed still couldn't quite imagine how much money a billion was, but it was clearly a lot of dollars. More dollars than there were stars in the sky. Suddenly Granny laughed.

"I told you it was a trick," she said.

"Please believe me. This is perfectly on the level, ma'am," Briggs said. "We are very, very serious."

"Boy oh boy," Granny said. "Yesterday it was some feller who thought he could fly. Today it's you boys sayin' you're gonna pay for that tar down in the swamp with more money than there is in all of creation!" She nudged Jed with her elbow. "I'm tellin' you, Jed. I think these fellers done lost their minds, but they don't know enough to miss 'em."

"I have the contract right here," Briggs said, opening his square leather case and taking out a long, white document that was many pages thick. He put the contract on the table. Jed stared at it, wondering what to do. He didn't want to admit to these men that he'd never learned to read.

"Well, I think I better sit and study on this for a while," he said.

Briggs gave him a knowing smile. "You want to obtain legal counsel. We understand. We'll be in touch."

"Fine," Jed said, relieved that he'd found a way to avoid admitting he couldn't read. "We'll talk to you then."

Briggs and Danforth started out of the shack. But then Briggs stopped and looked back at Jed.

"This is an awfully big deal and a very complicated procedure, Mr. Clampett," he said. "Are you sure you have someone smart enough to handle it?"

Jed rubbed his chin and glanced over at Granny, who was also deep in thought.

"All we got is Cousin Pearl's boy, Jethro," she said, shaking her head. "He's the only one with the learnin'."

"And just where did this Jethro get his learning?" Briggs asked skeptically.

"He went to school at Oxford," Elly May replied proudly.

"Oxford, you say?" Briggs's eyebrows went up. "A very good school indeed. Well, in that case we'll assume you're in good hands, Mr. Clampett."

Briggs and Danforth went out the door. Jed scratched his head and turned to Elly May and Granny.

"How do you like that?" he said. "Even them big city slickers have heard of Oxford. It must be a better school than we thought."

"I think the people of Oxford, Arkansas, ought to be right proud," Elly May said with a nod.

FIVE

Early the next afternoon, a beat-up old pickup truck with no front windshield or bumpers bounced over the rise behind the Clampett place and started down the hill toward the shack. Driving it was Jethro Bodine, a sturdy young man of twenty-two and a recent graduate of the Oxford, Arkansas, elementary school. Jethro was a big, handsome lad with black hair and a square

jaw. He had the sweet, happy-go-lucky smile of someone who had slightly less gray matter than most.

Seated beside him in the truck was his mother, Jed Clampett's cousin Pearl Bodine. Pearl was a neatly dressed woman who cared about appearances and considered herself to be the brightest of the entire Clampett clan, although some people said that wasn't much of a claim.

They started down the hill toward the Clampett shack. Pearl held on to her floppy, flowery hat as the wind whipped through the space where the windshield once was.

"Won't be long until we're at Uncle Jed's now," Jethro said gaily. "Too bad Jethrine ain't with us."

"Your twin sister has to study for the cosmetology test or she'll never get a job at Miss Jenny's beauty parlor," Pearl said. As the truck barreled downhill she could feel it picking up speed. Ahead she could see Jed's place, and the outhouse and chicken coop out back.

"Jethro, did you take care of those bare-as-bones brakes like I told you?" Pearl asked.

"Yes, Ma," Jethro replied. "I pulled 'em off the truck yesterday just like you said."

Pearl settled back and relaxed a little.

"Yup," Jethro said. "Them new brakes should be comin' in the mail next week."

Suddenly Pearl sat up straight. "Did I hear

you correctly, Jethro? Did you say the brakes were coming *next* week?"

"That's right, Ma."

"Then what's on the truck right now?" Pearl asked.

Jethro blinked. "Well, that there's a right good question, Ma."

The pickup was still gaining speed as it raced down the hill.

"How in the world do you expect to stop this thing if it ain't got no brakes?" Pearl asked in an agitated voice.

"Well, now, I guess I'll have to think about that," Jethro answered.

"You better think about it fast, boy," Pearl warned him. "Because we're about to crash."

The words were hardly out of her mouth when the pickup scattered a dozen chickens and smashed right into the outhouse, moving it several yards closer to the shack.

At the sound of the crash, Jed and Elly May came running out of the shack. Steam hissed from under the hood of the pickup and Jethro waved at them.

"Howdy, Uncle Jed. Howdy, Elly May."

Jed and Elly May waved back and went to inspect the damage to the outhouse. Meanwhile Jethro turned to his mother, whose eyes were still squeezed shut.

"You can open yer eyes, Ma," he said. "We're

here. And I must say we is sure lucky Uncle Jed knew to leave the outhouse just where my truck could crash into it."

Pearl opened her eyes in time to see the door to the outhouse swing open. Granny stormed out, hiking up her white bloomers. Her face was bright red and she was shaking her fist.

"Jethro Bodine!" she yelled. "Your head's emptier than last year's bird nest!"

But Pearl wasn't worried about Granny's fury. She knew the old lady would settle down. She hopped out of the pickup. News of her cousin's windfall had carried fast, and she already knew that he was about to become one of the richest men in the state, if not the whole country.

"I'm awfully sorry about the outhouse, Jed," she quickly apologized. "I promise you, Jethro will repair any damage he might have done."

"Well, it don't look too damaged to me," Jethro said as he took his time looking over the outhouse.

"Then the least he can do is move it back to where it was," Pearl offered.

"Tell you the truth, Pearl, I kinda like it in its new place," Jed said. "It gets a little chilly runnin' out here on them cold winter's nights. I always thought it might be a good idea to move the outhouse a little closer to the shack. Just never got around to doin' it, I guess."

"Well, then everything's fine," Pearl said with

a relieved smile. "I hope we're in time for Sunday supper."

"I ain't never known you to be late, Pearl," Granny snapped, and went into the shack.

Everyone went inside and sat down. The table was covered with pots of steaming wild greens and homemade stews, most of which had tails, claws, and snouts of various creatures sticking out. Jed sat at the head of the table. Elly May sat down opposite Jethro and Pearl. Everyone dug in while Granny scurried back and forth from the stove.

"I do declare," Pearl said with feigned innocence. "Seems like everything is always the same around here. I do wish something would change once in a while."

"Why, you know something's changed," Jethro said. "Uncle Jed here's become a rich man. Remember this morning, when you said you wanted to come over and give him some advice on how to spend all that money?"

Pearl smiled sheepishly and sank down a little in her chair. She loved her son, but he truly was an idiot.

"No surprises there," Granny said with a sigh, and shook her head.

"Well, I can't help it if news travels," Pearl said defensively.

"Heck, I don't mind, Granny," Jed said. "Even a billionaire can use some free advice. What's on your mind, Pearl?"

"Well, first I think you ought to have Jethro look over them contracts," Pearl said. "Then we'll talk."

They finished supper and cleared the table. Then Jed got out the contracts and showed them to Jethro.

"Shoot," Jethro said after a while. "If I was you, Uncle Jed, I'd sign these contracts right off."

"Why's that, Jethro?" Jed asked.

"All they's talkin' about is parties of the first part and parties of the second part," Jethro said. "Looks like they're fixin' to have a big shindig when you sign."

"No kiddin'?" Jed's bushy eyebrows rose. "You think maybe they're gonna try to make me pay for it?"

"I don't know," Jethro said. "Don't seem right that they'd give you a party and then make you pay for it."

"I reckon' you're right about that," Jed said. "Guess I might as well sign these here things. Granny, you got a pen?"

"Out in the back," Granny said.

Pearl frowned. "What's it doing out in back?"

"Holdin' the pigs in, what else?" Granny snapped.

"Not a *pig*pen, an ink pen," Pearl said. "So Jed can sign the contracts."

"Well, why didn't you say so?" Granny snapped

irritably. She'd always thought of Pearl as the uppity type.

"Well?" Pearl said.

"Well, what?" Granny said.

"Do you or do you not have an ink pen?"

"Now, what in the world would I be doing with an ink pen?" Granny replied.

"I think I've got one," Elly May said brightly. "It fell out of the pocket of that stranger who thought he could fly."

"Well, go get it, Elly May," Jed said. "And I'll sign these darn contracts and be done with it."

Elly May went to get the pen.

Pearl turned to Jed. "Jed, you're gonna be the richest man in these hills," she said. "Maybe in the whole state! You can have anything you want, do anything you like, go anyplace that strikes your fancy."

Jed frowned. "Why'd I want to do that?"

Pearl swept her arm dramatically around the shack. "Look at how you live. You're eight miles from your nearest neighbor. Your land is over-run with snakes and skunks. You use kerosene lamps for light. You cook on a wood stove summer and winter. You're drinking homemade moonshine and washing with homemade lye soap. You got no telephone, no TV, and no radio. And your bathroom is fifty feet from the house."

Jed couldn't help smiling proudly. "Yer right,

Pearl, we're livin' in paradise. Man'd have to be crazy to give all this up."

Granny nodded, but Pearl had something else in mind completely.

"Jed," she said, "you have no idea what's happened out there in the world in the past fifty years. Why, it's changed. People don't live like this anymore."

"They don't?" Jed scowled. "How do they live?"

"Oh, Jed, it's so hard to explain," Pearl said. It was such a different world out there. She thought a moment, trying to think of a way to explain it simply. Finally she said, "Jed, if I were you, I'd move to Californy."

"Californy?" Jed frowned.

"Yes, Jed," Pearl said. "If I had your money—"

"Which you *don't*," Granny reminded her.

"Well, if I did, I'd move to Beverly Hills," Pearl said.

"*Beverly* Hills?" Granny asked suspiciously. "What kind of name is that?"

"Beverly Hills is a place where they got movie stars and swimmin' pools," Pearl said, gushing. "They got fancy homes and limousines and the best restaurants in the world."

"I heard they got smog," Elly May added as she returned with the pen.

"What's a smog?" Granny asked.

Jethro's head went up. "Well, I reckon it's a small hog."

Jed took the pen from Elly May, but instead of signing the contracts, he just rubbed his chin thoughtfully. "Well, I don't know, Pearl."

"Let me tell you somethin', Jed Clampett," Pearl said, sitting down beside him at the table. "If you won't think of yourself, think about your daughter."

That surprised Jed. He looked over at Elly May, who'd picked up the baby goat again and was feeding it with the bottle. "What about her?"

"Well, look at her," Pearl said. "She ain't no little girl no more. When she walks, she bounces like twins stuffed in a pillowcase."

"Well, that ain't her fault," Jed said.

"Maybe it ain't," said Pearl. "But she needs a ma—someone to teach her womanly ways. Now, I reckon if you married one of them well-bred, refined Beverly Hills women, she could do it."

Deep inside, Jed knew she was right. And yet it was hard to think about changing. "Well, you know, Pearl," he said. "Granny's been doin' a pretty good job all these years. Right, Granny?"

To his surprise Granny hung her head and shook it slowly. "I hates to say it, Jed, but Pearl's right. I done what I could, but I cain't tame Elly May myself no more. She's runnin' wild now and ain't no different than a boy."

Over in the corner Elly May smiled and

puffed her chest out proudly. A button popped off her shirt and hit Jed in the eye.

"Well, I can think of *two* ways she's different," Jethro said.

"Now, you be quiet or I'll beat you till you're black and blue," Elly May threatened him.

"See what I mean?" Pearl asked. "Now, you take one of them refined Beverly Hills women—she could teach Elly May how to wear fancy dresses and act ladylike."

"That don't sound like much fun." Elly May pouted and got up.

"Where you goin', Elly May?" Jed asked.

"I'm just goin' outside to breathe a little fresh air before you folks all turn me into some kind of proper lady," she said.

Elly May went out the door, and Jed turned back to Pearl. "What's it like out in them Beverly Hills?"

"Oh, Jed, it's so beautiful," Pearl said dreamily. "The sun shines all the time and it never rains or snows."

"How can they have Christmas if it don't snow?" Granny asked.

"They make fake snow," Pearl said. "I read all about it. They got fake everything out there. Fake grass and fake snow and fake trees, so nothin' ever wears out."

Jed turned to Granny. "Bet they make it out of that there plastic stuff that young feller was blabbering about the other day." Pearl watched as Jed gave Granny a big wink to let her know he was joking. Granny winked back.

"Don't you go makin' fun of me, Jed," Pearl scolded him. "I am bein' deathly serious."

"Well, I appreciate your concern, Pearl," Jed said. "But it does seem to me that these here Beverly Hills is a mighty long ways to travel just to get hitched so that Elly May can learn to be ladylike. I mean, it takes me a day just to get around the lake."

"Well, for land's sake, Jed," Pearl said. "You cain't walk to Beverly Hills."

"You mean, I gotta ride that darn mule?" Jed asked.

"Heavens, no, Jed," said Pearl. "You got to drive. Why, Jethro could drive you out in his truck."

"Drive out with Jethro?" Granny sputtered. "I ain't drivin' nowhere with that dunderhead."

"Heck, Granny, I ain't no dunderhead," Jethro protested. "I done graduated me from sixth grade this year."

"Yeah, and it only took you twenty-two years to do it," Granny spat out.

"Now, Granny, that's not fair," Pearl said. "Jethro's the only one of us ever got past the first grade. It might have taken him a while, but that's because he's very meticulous."

"Meticulous?" Granny couldn't help smirking. "What's that? Another word for dumb?"

"Why, Granny, that's just plumb mean," Pearl said. "Jethro's a young man with an education. He deserves to see the world and fulfill his potential."

Granny watched as Jethro ladled his fifth helping of skunk stew into his bowl. "If that boy fills his potential any more, he's gonna go and split his pants."

Meanwhile Elly May had gone outside to feed her baby goat in peace. She surely didn't care for any of this talk about movin' to no hills named Beverly or havin' her pa marry some highfalutin lady who'd try and get her to act womanly.

Then she spotted a line of dust coming up the road. Why, it must be a car! But that was strange. The only people who ever came to their place by car were Pearl and Jethro, and they was already here!

Elly May put down the baby goat and slipped behind a tree. After a few moments the car pulled up at the edge of the property, and a feller got out and looked around. He walked up to the cabin and peeked in the window.

How do you like that? Elly May thought to herself. Her pa hadn't even signed them contracts, and those golddiggers were already startin' to snoop around. Well, she'd teach him a thing or two.

Quiet as a bobcat stalkin' chickens, she crept up behind him and threw on a full nelson.

"Hey!" the feller shouted, and tried to break Elly May's hold, but Elly May quickly rassled him to his knees.

"You give up?" she asked.

"Give up?" the man gasped. "Why should I give up? I'm not fighting."

Elly May tightened her grip.

"Ow! You're hurting me!" the man cried.

"Y'all gonna come peacefully?" Elly May asked.

"Yes," the man groaned. "I promise. Just ease up, okay?"

Elly May eased up all right. She eased that feller right up and slung him over her shoulder. Then she pushed through the front door of the shack.

Inside, everyone looked up, surprised. The wrinkles in Jed's forehead deepened.

"Elly May," he said. "Who you got there?"

"Caught him snoopin' round the shack, Pa," Elly May replied proudly.

"I'm from the oil company," the man stammered. "My name's Waters. Briggs sent me to see if you'd signed the contracts."

Jed knew this was no way to treat a bunch of fellers that wanted to make him a billionaire. "Elly May, put that man down."

Elly May let go.

Thud! The man fell to the floor and lay there in a heap. Jed bent down and helped him to his feet, then dusted him off a tad.

"Elly May," Granny screeched, "you're downright uncivilized."

"That's just what I've been talkin' about, Jed," Pearl said.

"But he was a stranger, Pa," Elly May said in defense.

Jed rubbed his stubbled chin. Maybe Pearl was right. Now that he was gonna be a billionaire, it didn't seem right that his daughter should go around throwing menfolk over her shoulder all the time. What kind of a future would a girl like that have? Yup, Jed could see that he was gonna have to make some sacrifices, and if it meant moving to them there Beverly Hills and finding a fancy wife to bring his daughter up right, he'd just have to go and do it.

"All right, I made my decision," he said, sitting back down at the table and picking up the pen. He signed the contracts. "For the good of this family, we're movin' to Beverly Hills!"

SIX

It only took a few days for Jed to settle his affairs. Then all the Clampetts' hillbilly neighbors and cousins pitched in to help load up Jethro's truck. Jethro, Jed, and Elly May stayed by the truck, tying things down, while the neighbors and cousins carried stuff out from the shack.

"Sure is nice that everyone's helpin' out, ain't it, Uncle Jed?" Jethro asked.

"Yup, although to tell you the truth, Jethro, I

sort of wish my cousins Hank and Frank had stayed home," Jed said. At that moment the two brutish-looking brothers came out of the shack carrying the kitchen table. They were wearing black-and-white skunk-skin caps and vests. Jed and Jethro had to hold their noses.

"Thanks, Hank. Thanks, Frank," Jethro said. "So how's the skunk-tanning business?"

"It stinks!" the brothers said, sharing a grin.

On the other side of the truck Elly May took the butter churn from a skinny man with red hair and freckles. His cheek bulged from a large chaw of tobacco, and he was carrying a tin cup.

"I'm gonna miss you, Spittin' Sam," Elly May said.

Spittin' Sam nodded and spit a big brown glob high into the air. *Plink!* He caught it in his cup.

"We're gonna miss you, too, Elly May," he said.

Elly May looked around at all her critters. The pigs and the muskrats and the goats all looked a little sad, as if they knew she was going away.

"I just don't know how they'll all get along without me," Elly May sniffed.

"Now, don't you worry, none, Elly May," Spittin' Sam said. "Me an' my boys'll take care of yer critters for ya."

Sam pointed back at his five boys, each one redheaded and the spittin' image of Spittin' Sam. They all spit in unison into their own cups.

Elly May managed a little smile. "Well, that sure is sweet of you, Sam."

"Like I said, Elly May, it's no problem," said Spittin' Sam. Instead of going back into the shack to get something else, he bent his head down and scuffed his boot against the ground. Elly May could tell there was something on his mind.

"What is it, Sam?" she asked.

"Well, nothin'," Sam said.

"Come on, Sam, you can tell me."

"Well, it's just that I heard you was goin' to Beverly Hills," Sam said.

"That's true," said Elly.

"Well, I know this is a mighty big favor to ask," Sam said, "but I was just wonderin' if maybe someday you could do a little favor for me."

"Sure, Sam, you know I'd do just about anything for you," Elly May said.

"Well, I done heard once that movie actor feller Sylvester Stallone lives out there, and I once seen one of his *Rambo* movies," Sam said. "I'll tell you, Elly May, it done changed my life. So I was just thinkin' how nice it would be, seein' how you and he are gonna be neighbors and all, if y'all would just stop and tell him that he has a real fan out here in the Ozarks."

"Aw, that's sweet, Sam," Elly May said with a smile. "I promise I'll do that just as soon as I see him."

"Gee, thanks, Elly May," Sam said. "And would you tell him that if he ever needs a feller in one of his movies who can spit in the air and catch it, I'm his man."

"I'll be sure and tell him," Elly May said.

Meanwhile the truck was starting to look pretty full.

"You think your new place in them there Beverly Hills will have room for all this?" Mayor Jasper asked.

"Well, I reckon so," Jed said.

"What kind of place you got out there?" asked Fat Elmer, who'd come to say good-bye.

"Well, I'm not really sure," Jed said. "Feller from the bank said he got me some sort of man shun. Don't know exactly what it is. I just hope they let women in, too."

It wasn't long before just about every Clampett possession was tied to the truck. It formed a small hill of furniture, suitcases, and odds and ends. Jed and Jethro had been careful to make sure it was well balanced so that the truck wouldn't tip over on turns.

"What about the chicken coop?" Elly May asked.

"Hmmm. Good question," said Jed. He turned to Pearl, who seemed to know more about life in Beverly Hills than anyone else. "What do you think, Pearl? Should we take the chicken coop or leave it here?"

Pearl pressed her lips together and thought. "I think I'd leave it, Jed. If you get out there and find you need one, you can always build another."

"I reckon you're right," Jed said. "Now, what about the outhouse?"

"I'm fairly certain you won't be needing it in Beverly Hills," Pearl said.

"Okay."

"Then it looks like we's about done packin'," Jethro said. "Guess it's time to go."

Jed nodded. All of a sudden he was struck by the enormity of what he was about to do. That there shack was the only home he'd ever known, and he'd never been beyond the hills. He walked off a little ways and stared out across the valley at the Ozark Mountains in the distance.

"Thank you, Lord, for blessin' me with these fine hills to live in all my life," he said humbly, taking his hat off and holding it in his hands. "Now you seen fit to make my cup overflow. I know I'll find the same kindhearted and friendly people in them there Beverly Hills as I've known here. . . ."

He paused and sighed and thought about his late wife. He'd now be leaving her, too.

"Katey," he said. "If you're listenin', you won't believe how big your baby, Elly May, has grown. I've tried my hardest to do what's best for her, but I ain't too proud to admit that I need

some help. Watch out over us and put in a good word when you can. I love you, Katey. Amen."

Jed stood for a moment more and looked out over the valley. Then Elly May joined him.

"Excuse me, Pa?"

"Yes, Elly May?"

"I think you got a problem with Granny."

Jed turned and raised a curious eyebrow. "Oh, yeah? How's that?"

"She says she ain't been more than ten miles from this here mountain in all her life and she weren't goin' nowhere now," Elly May said.

Jed took a deep breath. "I shoulda known we wouldn't get off without some kind of problem. Where is she?"

"Out by the still," Elly May said.

Jed walked around the back of the shack and found Granny sitting by the still in her rocking chair, an earthen jug by her side.

"What's all this 'bout you not goin' to Californy?" Jed asked.

"I'm stayin' here," Granny replied, sticking her chin out to let Jed know she was determined. "I don't see one good reason the Lord would want me aleavin' here now."

"Well, you know the Good Book says He moves in mysterious ways," Jed reminded her.

"Well, if *He* moves me, I'll go. But elsewise I'm stayin' right here."

Jed shoved his hands into his pockets. "Heck,

Granny, you know we've been talkin' about goin' for the most part of three days."

"Well, I'm stayin', Jed," she said. "I likes it here. Say what you will, but there's nothin' you can do to get me out of this rockin' chair."

As if to make sure Jed understood fully, she picked up her shotgun and laid it across her lap.

Elly May came around the shack. "What you gonna do?" she asked.

"Well, when Granny makes up her mind, there's nothin' you can do," Jed said with a shrug, and started back around the front of the house.

"But, Pa . . ." Elly May hurried after him.

"I reckon we'll just go," Jed said in a resigned tone.

"You ain't really gonna leave Granny, are you?" Elly May asked.

They got around to the front of the house. Jed stopped and winked at her. "'Course not. Now here's what we're gonna do. . . ."

He waved Jethro and a couple of the cousins over and huddled with them, whispering.

Suddenly they all raced around to the back of the house, picked up the rocking chair with Granny in it, and came running back. Before Granny could stop them, they'd lashed the rocking chair on top of all the other stuff in the back of the truck. Jed, Jethro, and Elly May jumped in the front seat.

"Get movin', boy!" Jed shouted. "Before she breaks loose!"

Just then Pearl ran up and reached over the truck door and gave her son a hug. "Take care, now!"

"Ya-hoo!" Jethro jammed the truck into gear and revved the engine. The truck backfired and started to roll. All of Jed's hillbilly cousins and neighbors lined up on either side of the truck, hooting and hollering. Then they raised their rifles and shotguns in the air and gave the Clampetts a twenty-five-gun salute.

Pow! Pow! Pow! Pow! . . .

Rifle fire filled the air. Moments later a dozen ducks plummeted to the earth, and the farewell celebration ended with hillbillies racing around, picking up the carcasses.

SEVEN

Rodeo Drive was splashed with sunlight. The pastel hues of the buildings lining the street glowed softly. Here were the choicest stores in the world, along with brokerage houses, insurance companies, and banks. One such bank was the Commerce Bank of Beverly Hills, housed in a massive marble building.

In the largest corner office on the second floor of the bank, Milburn Drysdale sat in a

large, black leather chair pushed up to a large, black lacquer desk. Drysdale was in his fifties, with perfectly trimmed hair and gold wire-rim glasses. His suit was conservative in cut and very expensive, and he had his shoes polished twice a day. He was a man who demanded perfection, both from himself and from those who worked for him.

On the wall behind his desk was a set of framed photos showing Drysdale with the important people he'd done business with, among them Burt Reynolds, Clint Eastwood, and Barbra Streisand. Set in the wall beside his desk was a large window so that the busy bank president could look out at his minions and make sure they, too, were busy.

Sitting across from him was his personal secretary, Jane Hathaway. Hathaway was in her forties and unmarried. She was a tall, slender woman with short, plain brown hair, given to wearing plain women's business suits and no makeup. Everything about her, from her sensibly low-heeled shoes to her extra-large briefcase, said that she was a serious, no-nonsense woman.

This morning Milburn Drysdale was particularly on edge. He'd just gotten the enormous billion-dollar Clampett account and he was determined to make sure that the Clampetts got the best treatment possible. Compounding his edginess was the recent behavior of one of his underlings, a young upstart named Woodrow Tyler.

"Tell me again what you heard?" he asked Hathaway.

"Apparently Woodrow Tyler knows about the Clampett account," his secretary reported. "He's been maneuvering to get his hands on it."

Drysdale nodded. There was nothing worse than allowing some green-gilled kid to get involved in an account as delicate and important as the Clampetts'.

"Has the escrow closed on the Clampett estate?" the bank president asked impatiently.

"Yes, chief," Hathaway replied. "With a cash offer of twenty-two million dollars, it closed rather quickly. I must say, it's rather inspirational how you managed to find a place for the Clampetts right next door to your own."

"The people who lived there were my best friends and neighbors for over twenty years," Drysdale replied. "I'm really going to miss them."

"It's a shame they had to file for bankruptcy and sell the place," Hathaway said.

"I know," Drysdale replied. "I'd hate to think that my phone call to the IRS had anything to do with it."

A moment of silence descended over the office. Then Drysdale cleared his throat.

"So what time does Clampett's flight arrive?"

"Uh, they're not coming by plane," Hathaway said a bit nervously. "They're driving."

"Driving?" Drysdale asked incredulously. "From Arkansas?"

"I know it makes no sense," Hathaway said.

"Well, not to you, perhaps," Drysdale said. "But to men of vision like myself, it's a sign of daring, self-confidence, vigor!"

In the large room outside the office, one of the least daring, least self-confident, and least vigorous employees of the Commerce Bank of Beverly Hills was talking furtively into his phone. His name was Woodrow Tyler and he was in his early thirties, with slicked-back black hair, a dark suit, and suspenders with large, green dollar signs on them. He was speaking quietly to his girl-friend, Laura.

"Okay," he whispered, thinking of her fabulous body. "I've got my hand on your butt."

"Can it, Woodrow." Laura sighed back through the phone. "I'm at the mall."

"You're naked, aren't you?" Woodrow Tyler said. "I can be there in five minutes."

"Are you always this desperate?" Laura asked with just the right amount of disgust in her voice.

"Yes," Tyler admitted, "but you've always said you admired that in a man."

"I hope you got the money from the Sloan account," Laura said. "Because I just maxed out your Visa card."

Tyler could imagine Laura at the moment: a gorgeous redhead with a great body in tight clothes, probably standing at a pay phone, surrounded by three or four clothing bags from the trendiest and most expensive stores in the mall.

"You know, Laura," he said. "Legally you're not allowed to use that card."

"Too late," Laura replied simply.

Tyler sighed. Laura was the most expensive woman he'd ever dated. But that was what made her so great!

"You'll be glad to know that I got four thousand dollars from the Sloan account," he said proudly.

But Laura's reaction was not what he'd hoped. "Only four thousand? Well, that'll keep me shopping for about a week."

Tyler winced. Her voice reeked of sarcasm. He knew he had to come up with something better.

"Listen," he said in a low voice. "I'm onto something much bigger. Our meal ticket is on its way from Arkansas even as we speak."

"Good," Laura snapped, "because before you get your hands on my butt, you'd better get your hands on some money."

Just the thought of his hands anywhere on her sent Tyler into his fantasy again "Okay," he said. "My hands are moving up your leg—"

Click! The line went dead. Tyler shook his head sadly. She'd hung up. Then suddenly his intercom burst on.

"Tyler! Get in here!"

Tyler sat up straight. It was Drysdale! He turned and saw the bank president waving at him through his office window.

"Yes, sir!" Tyler gasped into the intercom. He jumped up, stumbled over his chair, then hurried into the president's office. "You wanted to consult with me, sir? How may I be of assistance, sir?"

"Have a seat, Tyler," Drysdale said with a big smile, gesturing to a chair near the one where Hathaway sat. "Relax. Let's chat."

"Uh, very good, sir," Tyler said uncomfortably. "Chat away."

Drysdale stood over him. "I've heard you're quite excited about the arrival of J. D. Clampett."

Tyler made a conscious effort to appear relaxed. "Milburn, may I be the first to congratulate you on securing the Clampett account? I think that you and I together, the two of us, can really . . . er . . . exploit the potential of the Clampett financial portfolio."

"Hmmm." Drysdale rubbed his chin as if deep in thought. "You and I together. The two of us. Interesting. Go on."

Tyler opened a folder he'd brought with him. "I've already taken the liberty of drawing up power-of-attorney papers."

"Oh, have you?" Drysdale's eyebrows went up.

"Yes," Tyler said. "This way I can write checks, arrange investments, make international transactions. You know what I mean, sir. We'll really work the Clampett account. We'll be quite a team, sir." He leaned back in his chair, quite pleased with himself.

Drysdale paced around in front of him as if still deep in thought. "A team," the bank president mumbled.

Without warning Drysdale spun around and kicked Tyler's chair over. The younger man flipped head over heels and landed upside down in a ball. Drysdale stood menacingly over him.

"Tyler, you will personally rescind, shred, and burn every document you've drawn up with regard to the Clampetts!" he shouted.

"Uh, consider it done, sir," Tyler whimpered from the floor.

Drysdale turned to Hathaway. "Would you kindly remind Mr. Tyler of the first commandment of this bank."

"Thou shalt never do anything to show up the chief," Hathaway recited.

"Exactly," Drysdale said. "Tyler, do you know how I got the Clampett account?"

"Hard work, sir?" Tyler had rolled off his back and into a sitting position.

"Grow up, son," Drysdale said with a snicker. "It's because my wife Margaret's cousin Briggs

works for Ozark Mountain Oil. Therefore I will be handling the account personally."

"Duly noted, sir," Tyler said, getting up. "And nice kick, sir. Took me completely by surprise."

The young executive stepped over to the desk to retrieve the folder he'd carried in. As he reached for it he noticed another beside it, labeled CLAMPETT in large red letters. The folder looked important, so Tyler picked that one up, too. and headed out of the office.

"Uh, Mr. Tyler," Hathaway said.

"Yes?" Tyler stopped in the doorway.

"I believe you have inadvertently picked up the Clampett folder."

"No, I haven't." Tyler tried to hide the folder under the one he'd brought in.

"It's right there in your hand." Hathaway pointed.

"Oh, this?" Tyler pretended to be surprised. "So it is."

Hathaway took the Clampett folder from him and clutched it to her bosom as if it were a newborn baby. "Nice try, Tyler," she said with a smirk.

Once again Tyler headed for the door.

"One last thing," Drysdale said.

Tyler froze and turned. "Yes, sir?" he said meekly.

"The Clampetts are not to be badgered like garden-variety millionaires," said the bank's distinguished president. "They're billionaires. By definition they are people of discrimination, discernment, and refinement."

"Yes, sir!" Tyler started to salute, then remembered that Drysdale was not an army general. He turned and hurried out of the office. Drysdale and that dried-up prune, Hathaway, might have foiled his plans for the moment, but Tyler was nowhere near giving up. When you were talking about a billion dollars, there was plenty to go around for everyone.

EIGHT

A little while later the Clampetts were rolling down the freeway, agog at the sights Southern California offered. It had been an eye-opening trip from Arkansas, through Oklahoma City, then Amarillo in northern Texas and Albuquerque, New Mexico, where they saw real live Indians! Then they traveled through the petrified forest in Arizona, and past Flagstaff into the Mojave Desert past Needles, and finally into Los Angeles.

Jed had never realized how big the country was, or how many people were in it. Why, there on the freeway alone, literally thousands of cars were passing them in *both* directions. Jethro had never seen a road so wide. Truth was, until he left the Ozarks, he'd never seen a paved road either.

It was impossible to wave or say hello to everyone. Another strange thing was the way people constantly blew their horns.

"Hey, Jethro," Jed said. "Why do you think all them folks is blowin' them car horns so much?"

"Guess that's just the way they greet each other around here," Jethro replied. "What with all of them bein' in cars like this, they don't get the opportunity to say hello."

"Thing I cain't figure is how come none of the folks on the other side is honkin' at us," Jed said. "Seems like all the folks that's doin' the honkin' is behind us."

"Maybe we's goin' too slow," Elly May said. "Seems like an awful lot of folks is passin' us."

"Too slow?" Jed frowned. "How fast you figure you're goin', Jethro?"

"Well, the speedometer done broke back in the 1950s," Jethro said. "But if I had to guess, I'd say we're doin' about forty miles an hour."

"Forty?" Jed said. "Ooh-wee. I cain't imagine they're honkin' at us 'cause we're goin' too slow, Elly May. Forty's pretty darn fast."

"Well, all I can say is there's so many people here, it's gonna take a long time to meet everyone," Elly May said.

At that moment a young feller in a fast-looking black car raced around them. He yelled something they couldn't understand, then stuck his hand out his window. He made a fist and then extended his middle finger.

"Hey, Jethro," Jed said. "You know that feller who just pointed at you?"

"Cain't say I do," Jethro replied. "I reckon that's how they wave 'howdy' here in Californy."

Meanwhile Elly May had her face stuck in a map and was trying to match up the road names on the street signs with those on the map.

"Jethro!" she yelled. "I think this is where we turn off!"

Jethro quickly turned to the right, cutting across three lanes of traffic.

Screech! Several cars swerved out of the way to avoid crashing into Jethro's overloaded pickup truck, including a dented yellow Camaro with darkly tinted windows.

Beeeeeeppppp! The Camaro blared its horn.

"Guess he's sayin' hello," Jethro said as he and the yellow Camaro stopped at a stop sign.

"Then I reckon we ought to say hello back," said Jed. Both he and Jethro made fists and extended their middle fingers. A moment later one of the Camaro's windows went down. Inside, a young man wearing a sweat-stained red bandanna stuck his arm out, flashing a black automatic pistol at them.

"Yo, chump," the young man said with a sneer.

"Hey, looky there," Granny said. "Jed, that feller wants to show off his gun to you."

"Ain't that right neighborly," Jed said, leaning over toward the young man. "That's a mighty nice gun you got there, son. Here's what I carry."

Jed lifted up his big double-barrel shotgun. Granny held up her shotgun, too. The young man's eyes went wide.

Screech! The Camaro quickly took off.

"Guess he must've had someplace important to go," Jed said.

Not far away Milburn Drysdale stood on the balcony of his mansion and gazed over the tall stone wall at the estate that now belonged to the bank's newest and most wealthy client, J. D. Clampett. Drysdale had come home to have lunch with his wife, but it was also a good opportunity to make sure things were going according to plan.

The estate was on a rectangular piece of property of roughly four and a half acres. There was a broad front lawn with fountains and a long, narrow driveway, which led up to a circle before the front door. Then there was the mansion itself,

made of tan sandstone and rising fortresslike for three floors. Behind that were more lawns and gardens—and the pool and tennis courts, of course.

A small red Miata sports car was parked in the driveway in front of the house. Drysdale knew the car belonged to Hathaway, and as he gazed over the lawns he spotted her in the back of the mansion measuring the height of the grass with a ruler.

He watched as she straightened up and withdrew a small cellular phone from her leather briefcase. A second later the portable phone in Drysdale's bedroom rang. Drysdale stepped inside and picked it up.

"Greetings, chief! Hathaway checking in."

"Good afternoon, Hathaway," the bank president said as he strolled back out to the balcony. "Is everything set?"

"I can happily report that the mantle of responsibility you have draped on my shoulders is in no danger of slipping off," Hathaway announced.

"Excellent." Drysdale waved to her from his balcony. She immediately saluted back.

"Please, Hathaway," Drysdale said into the portable phone. "Don't salute. It's embarrassing."

He hung up the phone and walked inside the house. There were more preparations necessary to ensure that J. D. Clampett would be happy as a client of the Commerce Bank of Beverly Hills. Drysdale went down the steps to the living room, where his sixteen-year-old son, Morgan, was reclining on a sofa, staring at a large television set with MTV turned up loud.

Drysdale stepped up to the couch, took the remote, and flicked the television off.

"What'd you do that for?" Morgan whined.

"I did that because it is another beautiful California day, and as far as I can tell, you've done nothing except stare at that television since you got up."

"Sure, but I didn't get up until noon, so it's only been half an hour," Morgan complained.

Drysdale sighed. "Where is your mother?"

"She's changing."

"That would be too much to hope for," Drysdale said dryly.

"Huh?" Morgan frowned. "I'm serious, Dad. She really is changing her clothes."

"Yes, yes," Drysdale said. "You see, it was a joke, Morgan. Something you would need a sense of humor to appreciate."

A door opened and Drysdale's wife, Margaret, swept into the room. She was in her late forties, and the aging process was catching up to her, although she was fighting it tooth and nail. She was followed into the room by Babette, her large white poodle whose hair was cut into pom-poms on her tail, legs, body, and head.

Grrrrrrr . . . Babette growled when she saw Drysdale.

"Oh, Milburn." Margaret looked surprised to find her husband home. "What are you doing here?"

"We have a lunch date, remember?" Milburn said.

"Oh, dear. I'm afraid I'll have to cancel. I just haven't been spending enough quality time with Babette."

Quality time with a *dog*? Had Drysdale heard this from anyone else, he wouldn't have believed it. Unfortunately it was his wife who said it, so it was quite believable. He felt his teeth grind, but he managed to put a smile on his lips.

"Margaret, dear, we're trying to do more things together, remember?" he said. "We're trying to put the spark back. So get your liposuctioned butt in gear, or else we're moving to the Valley!"

Margaret blinked quickly. "I'll meet you at the car, dear."

Morgan was reaching for the remote again, but Drysdale turned and grabbed it away from him. "Morgan, I have a job for you."

"A job?" Morgan's voice cracked. He appeared to be truly terror-stricken by the thought.

"J. D. Clampett has a daughter your age," the bank president said. "Starting Monday she'll be attending Beverly Hills High. I want you to show her around and be her friend."

"You're going to *pay* me to hang out with this girl?" Morgan shook his head. "Forget it, Dad, she must be a major bowwow."

Just as he'd done with his wife, Drysdale decided to get his son in line. "Morgan, close your eyes and picture this—I cut off your allowance, cancel your credit cards, and delete you from my will. Now, how do you see yourself in the future?"

"Uh, grilling frozen cow parts at Burger King?" Morgan guessed.

Drysdale smiled. "I can't imagine why people say you're stupid, my boy. You appear very intelligent to me."

"Okay, Monday morning, first period, eight A.M.," Morgan said with a resigned sigh. "I'll be her friend. She'll be just like my little sister—the one Mom didn't have because she was certain it would ruin her figure."

Jethro turned the truck around a corner, and the Clampetts found themselves on a broad street lined with tall palm trees and large houses.

"Stop the car, Jethro!" Granny suddenly shouted.

Jethro jammed on the brakes. "What is it, Granny?"

"Roadkill." Granny pointed at a squirrel carcass lying in the middle of the street. "Looks pretty fresh. Cain't just leave it there."

"You're right about that, Granny," Jed said, rubbing his empty stomach. "Roadkill stew sounds mighty good right about now."

Granny climbed down from the pickup and pulled an old shovel out of the back. She was walking across the street when a cream-colored Rolls-Royce Corniche convertible skidded to a stop just a few feet before her. The driver pressed on his horn and shook his fist.

Granny glared at the man driving the car and waved her shovel angrily. "Oh, no, you don't, you old coot. I seen it first."

It didn't look to Jed like the feller in the car was in such a rush to take Granny's roadkill. "Easy now, Granny," he said. "Maybe that feller's bein' neighborly like them nice folks we met on that extra-wide road."

"Yeah," said Jethro. "What do you say we give these folks a nice Californy howdy."

The Clampetts all smiled at the man and his wife, then made fists and raised their middle fingers. The man gave them the finger back.

This confirmed what Jed already suspected.

"See, Granny?" he said. "These Beverly Hills folks are down-home cordial."

"I reckon you're right, Jed," Granny replied. She scooped up the dead squirrel in her shovel and held it up for the folks in the other car to see. "I'm sure there's plenty here for all of us."

"How revolting!" the woman in the car cried.

"Suit yourself," Granny said with a shrug. She walked over to the truck and flipped the dead squirrel into a pot containing a couple of dead snakes, prairie dogs, and an armadillo they'd picked up along the road in Texas. Then she climbed onto the truck and Jethro jammed it back into gear.

In his Rolls, Milburn Drysdale and his wife watched as the truck backfired and groaned and slowly started off. Margaret quickly yanked up the car's telephone and handed it to her husband.

"Don't just sit there, Milburn," she said. "Call Westec Security. There are vagabonds prowling the streets!"

While Drysdale made the call to the private security force that patrolled Beverly Hills, the Clampetts approached their new home. The tall metal gate that protected the property had been left open for their arrival. Jethro stopped at the entrance. They all stared down the long driveway, past the fountains, to the huge mansion.

"This cain't be the right place," Jed said.

"You reckon we're at the wrong spot?" Jethro asked.

"But, Pa!" said Elly May. "It's the right address."

"You sure you ain't made some mistake, Elly May?" Granny asked.

"I swear," said Elly May. "It's writ down right here. Five, one, eight, C-R-E-S-T-V-I-E-W D-R-I-V-E." She pointed at the telegram, which had arrived at the shack the day before they left.

"Well, I reckon it cain't hurt to take a little peek," Jed said. "Go on, Jethro."

Jethro drove the truck through the gate.

"That ain't no house," Granny said as they got closer. "It's most likely a government building chockful of revenuers. I say we skedaddle quick before we end up on the chain gang."

"You think she's right?" Jethro asked.

"I'm tellin' you, Pa," Elly May insisted. "This is the address."

Jed rubbed his chin. "Well, if this is a government building, it sure is quiet. What say we reconnoiter?"

Jethro stopped the truck and they got out. Jed picked up his shotgun. Duke tagged along beside him as he stepped up the path from the driveway to the front door.

"Look, Pa," said Elly May. "They left the front door ajar."

Jed gently pushed the front door open and they all stared inside at the most elegant interior most people had ever seen. A double marble staircase curved down from upstairs. Statues of naked men and women posed in alcoves, and the walls were covered with large, priceless pieces of art.

"Well, doggies," Jed whispered. "Whatcha think, Duke?"

Aaaahhhhooou! Duke let out a howl.

"Maybe he smells something upstairs," Jethro said, taking the marble steps two at a time to see.

The rest of the Clampetts stayed downstairs. Granny bent down and ran her hand over the white marble floor. "Why, they ain't even put down the floorboards," she said in disgust. "This ain't nothin' but a cold slab floor."

"Hey, Uncle Jed, guess what?" Jethro called from the second floor. "There's a whole 'nother house up here!"

"Well, then you better come on down," Jed said. "It's pretty likely that house belongs to someone else."

The Clampetts wandered around the foyer looking at the art and antiques.

"Amazin'," Jed muttered. He'd never seen anything like it.

"Hey, Pa?" Elly May said. "Why do you reckon they got two sets of steps?"

"Why, heck, anybody knows that," Jethro said. "One's for goin' up, and the other's for goin' down."

Now a fluffy white creature with hair shaped like balls scampered into the Clampett mansion.

Duke turned to face the creature, and their noses touched as they sniffed each other. Both tails started to wag happily.

"What a pretty critter." Elly May gushed and knelt to pet it.

"What kind of critter you think that is?" Jethro asked.

"Cain't say I know," Jed said. "Looks mighty strange to me."

"Well, she may look strange," Elly May said. "But it looks to me like Duke's got a new friend."

The Clampetts didn't know it, but they were not alone in the mansion. Hathaway had heard them enter. Now she dialed the police on her cellular phone and whispered, "Hello, this is Jane Hathaway. I wish to report the unlawful entry of a gang of armed and dangerous hooligans at the Clampett estate. Five, one, eight Crestview Drive. I need you here Code Three, and I will be timing you."

Hathaway hung up, but she knew she couldn't stop there. It was her sworn responsibility to protect and defend the Clampett property in all eventualities. She took a deep breath and steeled herself to the possibility of horrible physical harm to her being, and then strode forthrightly through the French doors into the living room.

"Cease and desist, everyone!" she shouted.

Then, pointing at Jed, she said, "If I were you, sir, I'd yield, submit, and capitulate. Justice is about to descend like an angry rain upon your larcenous head."

Jed and the others looked up at the ceiling. "I'm sorry, ma'am, but that ceiling looks pretty solid to me. I don't see no way for much rain to get in."

"Well, it was just a matter of speech," Hathaway admitted. "I didn't see no rain clouds when we was comin' in," said Granny.

"No, you don't understand," Hathaway tried to explain. "It was just a simile. I didn't mean it was really going to rain."

"Then why'd you say it?" Granny wanted to know.

Hathaway was starting to wonder just what sort of hooligans these people were. Why were they arguing about semantics? Perhaps they weren't as dangerous as she'd thought.

"Because I was trying to convey a warning to you," she said. "It had nothing to do with rain."

"Well, I never heard of someone sayin' it was gonna rain and then changin' their minds so fast," Granny said.

"All right, enough!" Hathaway was exasperated. "I would like to know what you desperadoes are doing in this house."

"Well, that's a mighty long story," Jed said.

"But he don't mind tellin' it," Granny added.

"Pa was huntin' one day with ol' Duke," Elly May said.

"And Duke spotted this big ol' jackrabbit," said Jethro.

"So I takes aim and I gits ready to fire," Jed said, raising his shotgun to demonstrate what happened. Expecting the worst, Hathaway threw up her arms.

"Don't shoot!" she cried.

"Pardon, ma'am?" Jed said, lowering the gun.

But Hathaway didn't reply. She was staring past them through the open front door. Outside, she could see four Beverly Hills Police Department squad cars racing up the driveway, followed by two black-and-white Westec Security cars. The police parked their cars in a circle around the front of the house and then jumped out and hid behind them.

One of the cops aimed a loudspeaker toward the house. "Attention inside! This is the Beverly Hills Police Department. You are surrounded! Drop your weapons and file out one at a time."

"Don't shoot!" Hathaway shouted to the police. "They've taken me hostage."

The Clampetts went over to a large picture window that looked out over the vast front lawn. They watched curiously as the police crouched behind the cars with their guns drawn.

"Attention inside," the cop with the loud-speaker shouted again. "Drop your weapons and file out one at a time. This is the Beverly Hills Police Department."

"I *told* you this weren't no house," Granny said. "You heard him. This is the Beverly Hills Police Department."

"Now you can tell your story to the law," Hathaway said righteously.

"Well, if they'd enjoy hearin' it, I reckon we could," Jed said, hitching his thumbs through his belt loops.

"This is your last warning," the cop with the loudspeaker shouted. "Come out with your hands up."

"You think we should?" Jethro asked.

"Go out there with our hands up?" Jed said. "Naw, that's just plain silly. If they want me to tell 'em my story, they should just come in here and set down."

Bang! It sounded like someone had fired a shot. A moment later a smoking teargas canister bounced through the open door and clattered across the marble floor.

"Look, Pa!" Elly May cried. "They's playin' kick the can!"

She ran up and kicked the can hard, right back through the door. Through the window, the Clampetts watched the canister fly back among the police cars and suddenly explode. In a flash men in dark blue uniforms were running in all directions, coughing and rubbing their tearing eyes.

"That was one strange can," Jed muttered.

Hathaway watched the policemen scatter. Was all lost? she wondered.

As Woodrow Tyler walked up the concrete steps to the small bungalow he and Laura shared, he pulled his tie loose and thought about all that money J. D. Clampett would never miss. What was a million or two to a billionaire? Mere pocket change.

Tyler pushed open the door and went inside. The bungalow was tiny and barely furnished. There was a bed, a television, a table, and two chairs. The walls were bare, as was the cupboard, but Tyler was confident all that would soon change.

Inside, Tyler beheld a lovely sight. Across the room, in front of the bungalow's only closet, Laura stood with her back to him, putting away the results of her latest shopping spree. She was surrounded by shopping bags, and the closet was already filled with her clothes. As Tyler watched she reached up to put a new sweater on the closet's highest shelf. In the act of reaching up, her tight and extremely short leather skirt rode high up, providing a delightful glimpse of her shapely derriere.

Feeling instantly inspired, Tyler quickly slipped off his pants, revealing a pair of white boxer shorts adorned with little smiley faces.

"Honey, I'm home," he called. "Why don't you come over here and give your little embezzling cowboy a ride around the bungalow?"

Laura looked over her shoulder at him, looking completely unamused. "No."

"Aw, why not?" Tyler asked, still hopeful.

"Because I'm living in this dump when I should be living in a mansion in Beverly Hills," Laura replied coldly.

"Laura, honey, I've explained this to you before," Tyler said. "You *do* live in Beverly Hills. Bungalows three-A, three-B, and three-C are in Los Angeles. But the city line goes through three-D, which means that technically, since this is three-G, we live in Beverly Hills."

"*Technically?*" Laura finished putting her new clothes away and shut the closet door. "Who cares about *technically*? *Technically* doesn't get me a pool and a tennis court. *Technically* doesn't get me invited to Jack Nicholson's next party. *Technically* isn't worth squat, Woodrow."

Tyler sighed. He could see that Laura was in no mood to fulfill his fantasies. He walked over to a tiny cabinet and put his pants away.

"Look, Laura, you have to believe me," he said. "Pretty soon you're going to have everything your heart desires."

"Do you know how many times you've said that to me?" Laura asked. "You're all talk, Woodrow. All promise, but no delivery. I bet

you've forgotten that you said we'd have enough money to buy me a baby-sealskin coat this month."

She walked into the bathroom and shut the door behind her. Tyler stepped up to the door and tried the knob, but it was locked. Darn, he thought.

"Listen to me, honey," he said. "Pretty soon we'll have enough money to fly to wherever those seals are and club them to death ourselves."

"Promises, promises," Laura muttered from inside the bathroom.

Tyler pressed his ear to the door and tried to listen. He wondered what wonderful things she was doing in there. Suddenly the bathroom door flew open. Tyler lost his balance and stumbled inside, banging his head on the toilet bowl.

"You're sick," Laura said contemptuously.

Tyler looked up and saw that she'd changed into a skintight workout leotard that outlined every inch of her fabulous body.

"Not sick!" Tyler gasped. "Just . . . attentive."

He scrambled to his feet and followed Laura back into the bungalow. She walked over to the TV and slid a workout tape into the VCR. A workout video called "Buns of Steel" came on.

"And worshipful," Tyler added as he watched Laura get down on her hands and knees on the floor and begin to do donkey kicks in time to the music.

"Don't drool," Laura said, looking at him over her shoulder.

Tyler straightened up. "This time the promise is going to come true. We're going to be rich."

"Oh, sure."

"We will," Tyler insisted. "J. D. Clampett, the billionaire, just opened up an account at the bank. And guess who Drysdale said should handle his financial affairs personally?"

Tyler pointed at himself. It hardly mattered to him at the moment that what he'd just said was an enormous lie, just so long as Laura believed it enough to stay around.

"So who is this Clampett guy?" Laura asked. "If he's so rich, how come I've never heard of him?"

"He just made a sudden killing in the oil business," Tyler explained. "Now he has more money than he knows what to do with."

"Really?"

"Honest Injun," Tyler said with a smile.

Laura looked over her shoulder at him. Only this time she licked her lips and made her eyes wide and inviting.

"You know, it's a real problem for these guys when they have more money than they know what to do with," Tyler said with a knowing smile.

"And it's a problem I think we can help him with," Laura said, her voice soft and sexy. "I

really think you should find out more about J. D. Clampett."

"And if I do?" Tyler asked.

"I might just consider giving you that little ride around the bungalow you want so much," Laura replied.

NINE

With the arrival of more than a dozen backup officers, the Clampetts were finally arrested and taken to the Beverly Hills Police Department, where they were put in the lineup room along with two young men in Armani suits and an outraged former movie queen with billowing blond hair. Everyone stood in profile. Jed, Jethro, Elly May, and Granny all stared down at their hands, which were covered with black fingerprinting ink.

Drysdale and Hathaway stood behind a glass partition on the other side of the room.

"Have you arranged for the house to be taken care of?" Drysdale asked.

"Yes, chief," Hathaway answered. "I've got a cleaning crew in there right now wiping away any trace of mayhem these hooligans may have left behind."

"Good, good," Drysdale said. "The last thing I want is for J. D. Clampett to get any wind of this."

"So far none of the local newspapers, radio, or TV stations know," Hathaway reported. "But should they find out, I've got damage control on alert. Anyone who runs the story will be in danger of losing a great deal of Commerce Bank advertising."

"Very good." Drysdale smiled. "I think you've successfully avoided a potential disaster. I look forward to seeing J. D. Clampett come to town without the slightest suspicion that anything went wrong."

A burly police captain named Gallo joined them behind the partition. "We've ID'd them all."

"Excellent." Drysdale nodded.

"We want the wheels of justice to spin quickly," Hathaway said. "These criminals must be prosecuted and incarcerated before our client has an opportunity to learn about this unfortunate incident. The reputation of Milburn Drysdale is at stake."

The police captain frowned. "Who's Milburn Drysdale?"

Drysdale cleared his throat.

"Oh, it's you," Captain Gallo said. "Well, I don't know what kind of reputation you have at stake, but we'll do our best. We don't want these kind of people roaming around Beverly Hills, either."

The police captain leaned toward a mike and spoke into it. "Would everyone please turn to your left?"

Everyone turned to face the window except Jethro, who turned to face the wall.

"Uh, would someone tell that gentleman that he turned to the right?" Gallo asked.

Jed tapped Jethro on the shoulder, and he turned toward the window with a sheepish grin on his face. "Sorry 'bout that."

Granny reached into her sweater and took a swig from her flask. "I knew we shouldn'ta never left home. I knew it, I knew it, I knew it."

"Now, now, Granny," Jed said. "We'll just have to get to the bottom of this and see what it's about."

"Well, I sure hopes we get to the bottom of it before I get to the bottom of *this*," Granny said, holding up her flask.

"Excuse me," Captain Gallo said, "but drinking is not permitted during the line up."

"Sorry." Granny slipped the flask back into her pocket.

"Okay," Gallo said, reading from a clipboard. "From left to right, we have the following—Jedediah Clampett, Jethro Bodine, Elly May Clampett, and Daisy May Moses, aka Granny."

THUD! Milburn Drysdale dropped heavily into the chair behind him and appeared dazed.

"Chief! Chief!" Hathaway cried. "Are you all right?"

Drysdale didn't respond. Hathaway began to dig frantically through her purse.

"Should I get smelling salts?" Captain Gallo asked.

"No!"

"How about water?"

"No!" Hathaway shook her head. "He needs this!" She pulled a thick wad of bills out of her purse and fanned it under the bank president's nose.

Drysdale blinked.

"Say something, chief!" Hathaway gasped. "Say anything!"

Drysdale's eyes came into focus. "You're fired!"

Hathaway's eyes went wide and her heart

skipped several beats. She staggered backward and crumpled against a wall.

"Gee, all she was trying to do was revive you," Captain Gallo said as Drysdale got to his feet. "Firing her seems awful harsh."

"I'd appreciate it if you'd mind your own business," Drysdale snapped. "Now, release those people at once."

"But they're under arrest," Gallo said.

"They *were* under arrest," Drysdale corrected him. "We are dropping all charges immediately."

"Well, you can't do that, sir," Captain Gallo said. "The charges can only be dropped by the owner of the property."

"He *is* the owner of the property!" Drysdale snapped, pointing at Jed.

"You're telling me that guy owns a twenty-million-dollar estate on Crestview Drive?" Captain Gallo asked in wonder. "Look at the way he's dressed."

"It's called *grunge*," Drysdale replied dryly. "It's a very popular look among the well-heeled these days."

"Well, you can call it whatever you want," the police captain said. "But they still look like a bunch of hillbillies fresh from the Ozarks to me."

"I appreciate your opinion," Drysdale said. "Now please release them."

*   *   *

A few minutes later Jed and the others stepped out of the Beverly Hills police station and into the bright California sunshine. Jed rested his shotgun over his shoulder and Jethro rubbed the fingerprinting ink off his hands with a paper towel.

"Well, that sure was an unusual way of greetin' us," he said.

"If that's the way they treat good folks around here, I'd sure hate to see what they do to criminals," Granny said.

"Mr. Clampett?"

Jed turned and saw a well-dressed man and a woman standing behind him. "That's me," he said with a smile.

The man took Jed's hand and shook it. "Milburn Drysdale, president of the Commerce Bank of Beverly Hills."

"Sounds familiar," Jed said.

"It should," said Drysdale. "We've got all your money. Er, I should say, we're holding it for you."

"Oh, right," said Jed. "Well, thanks for doin' that. You know, I was thinkin' about how many mattresses I'd need to hide a billion dollars. I reckon I'd need a house about the size of the one we was in before to store all them mattresses. So I really appreciate you folks holdin' all the money for us."

"It's no problem, really," Drysdale said. "And

I just wanted to tell you how deeply sorry I am for any embarrassment my former assistant, Jane Hathaway, may have caused you."

Drysdale pulled Hathaway forward by the arm.

"I do humbly apologize for my egregious error." Hathaway sniffed. "Rest assured that it will never happen again since I am no longer in the employ of the bank."

Drysdale nodded approvingly, and Hathaway turned to him.

"I'll clean out my desk at once, Mr. Drysdale," she said. She turned away and accidentally bumped into Jethro, spilling the contents of her briefcase on the ground. Flustered, she kneeled down to gather up her papers. Jed and Jethro knelt down to help her.

"Oh, it's really not necessary for you to help me," Hathaway said. "I can do it myself. Really."

"So, uh, then I'll assume everything is fine," Drysdale said.

Jed was so busy helping Hathaway that he didn't realize Drysdale was addressing him. Suddenly the bank president fell to his knees, clutching Jed by the leg.

"Please, Mr. Clampett," he begged. *"Please* don't take your money from my bank. I'll do anything you want. I'll contribute to charity. I'll eat mud. *Anything!"*

Granny and Elly May watched, amazed. "I

ain't seen beggin' like that since the day I caught them revenuers tryin' to take down my still and I threatened to shoot 'em."

Jed straightened up and grabbed Drysdale by the collar, pulling him up as well.

"You don't have to eat no mud," Jed told him. "Why, look at all the fancy restaurants they got around here."

"But the money," Drysdale gasped.

"Well, all I want is for this here lady to watch over my affairs," Jed said, gesturing toward Hathaway.

"Me?" Hathaway said, stunned. "You want *me*?"

"There's no need to be hasty about these things," Drysdale quickly said. "There are many people still employed at the Commerce Bank of Beverly Hills who are quite capable of—"

"I'm sure there are," Jed said. "But I reckon this here lady did what she did because she didn't know who we were."

"Yes, that's quite true," Drysdale said. "Believe me, Mr. Clampett, if she'd had any idea who you were, this never would have happened."

"Well, that's just the point," Jed said.

Drysdale frowned. "I'm afraid I'm not following you, sir."

"It's like this," Jed said. "We're the Clampetts. But if we weren't who we are, I'd be much obliged to this lady for doin' what she did."

"Uh, could you repeat that, Uncle Jed?" Jethro said, scratching his head.

"It's simple, Jethro," Elly May said. "We're who we are. But if we wasn't who we are, then we'd be someone else. And if we was someone else, then this here Hathaway was right to do what she did."

Hathaway straightened up and regained her composure. It had been some time since anyone had complimented her on a job well done.

"So if I wasn't me, I'd be someone else," Jethro said.

"That's right," Elly May said.

"But maybe I'd be my sister, Jethrine," Jethro said. "Then I wouldn't be me, but I'd still be a Bodine. And that's almost like bein' me."

The Clampetts glanced at each other and scowled.

"We'll discuss this some more later, Jethro," Jed said. Then he turned to Hathaway. "In the meantime, what do you say?"

"I don't know what to say," Hathaway said. "Except, Mr. Clampett, that I'll work hard for you."

"I trust you will," Jed said. He turned back to the bank president. "Is that all right with you, Mr. Drysdale?"

"It's exactly what I would do in your situation," Drysdale said solemnly.

"Then it's agreed," Jed said. As was the hill-

billy custom, he spit in his hand and held it out to the bank president. Drysdale stared at Jed's outstretched hand in horror. But a billion dollars was at stake, so Milburn Drysdale spit in his own hand and shook Jed's.

When they'd finished, Granny came over and stood up on her tiptoes to whisper something in Jed's ear. Jed listened to Granny and nodded.

"Now, Granny just made a very nice suggestion," he said. "Mr. Drysdale, to show there's no hard feelin's about you havin' us arrested and put in jail on our first day in these here Beverly Hills, we'd like it if you and your family would come by for Sunday supper tomorrow."

"Why, that's a very kind offer," Drysdale said. "We'll be delighted to accept."

"It'll be a good opportunity for me to swap recipes with your wife," Granny said.

Drysdale seemed to grimace slightly. "Yes, uh, Ms. Moses," he said. "I'm sure my wife would like that."

A long, white stretch limousine pulled up to the curb. The only thing Jed had ever seen that resembled it was a hearse. He took off his hat and pressed it to his chest. Then he and the other Clampetts bowed reverently.

"What are you doing?" Drysdale asked.

"Well, we always pay our respects," Jed said.

"Respects to what?" Drysdale asked.

"Why, the dead, of course," Jed said.

Drysdale looked at the limo and back at Jed. "Let me explain. This is a limousine. It's going to take you home."

Jethro stepped closer and peeked inside, "Hey, Jed, looky here! It's got a little house in it!"

"A house?" Drysdale frowned.

"Sure," said Jethro. "There's a TV and a telephone and a refrigerator and glasses. Guess it must be one of them there mobile homes."

"No, no," said Drysdale. "It's just a limo. It's sole purpose is to get you from one place to another comfortably."

"You sure nobody lives in it?" Jethro asked.

"Yes, quite sure," Drysdale replied. "Now you go along. I'll follow you in my Rolls."

The limo's uniformed driver, wearing dark sunglasses and a hat, came around and opened the door for them. Jethro ducked his head and started to climb into the limo, then quickly backed out and gave the driver a suspicious look.

"What's the problem, Jethro?" Jed asked.

"This ain't no trick, is it?" Jethro asked.

"What do you mean?" Drysdale asked.

"Well, this here uniformed feller," Jethro said. "He ain't takin' us off to some other jail, is he?"

"No, no, of course not," Drysdale said. "He's simply your driver."

"Then why's he all dressed up like that?" Jethro asked.

"Because that's the way limousine drivers dress," Drysdale said.

Granny stepped up to the driver and gave him a look from head to toe. "I reckon maybe you could get a job as a limousine driver," she said to Jethro. "You'd look good in one of these here uniforms."

"Yer right, Granny," Jethro said. "Maybe I will. Seems like these here Beverly Hills are a pretty expensive place to live. I might need me some spendin' money."

Drysdale rolled his eyes and muttered something about someone having no idea what they were worth.

"Uh, excuse me, chief," Hathaway said a bit timidly. "My car is still on the Clampett grounds."

"Well, then call a cab," Drysdale snapped.

"Come along with us," Granny said as she got into the limousine. "We've got more than enough room in this here cemetery wagon."

"Why, that's very nice of you," Hathaway said with a smile. "Thank you, Ms. Moses."

"You kin call me Granny," Granny said. "That's what everybody's called me since I was little."

"Oh, come on," Hathaway said. "You haven't looked like this since you were little."

"Oh, she sure has," Elly May said. "Why, my pa says Granny ain't aged a day in fifty years."

Hathaway followed Granny into the limo. Jethro was looking over at Drysdale's Rolls.

"Ain't that a fancy car," he said. "What kind is it?"

"Why, it's a Rolls," Drysdale replied.

"Just rolls along, huh?" Jethro grinned.

"Very smoothly and quietly," Drysdale said a bit proudly.

"Bet it ain't like my pickup truck," Jethro said.

"No, I rather doubt that it is," said Drysdale.

"Think I could drive it?" Jethro asked suddenly. "I mean, now that we're neighbors?"

Drysdale's jaw dropped. His Rolls Royce Corniche? His pride and joy? Driven by that simpleton? "You . . ." he stammered, "want to drive my one-hundred-and-eighty-thousand-dollar Rolls-Royce?"

Jethro stared at the bank president with a dumb grin plastered on his face. Drysdale turned and glanced at Jed, who nodded almost imperceptibly.

"Of course you can drive it," Drysdale said, forcing a wooden smile onto his face. "Why, that's a great idea!"

Jethro took off toward the Rolls like an excited child. Drysdale walked quickly after him. Jed got into the limo, and the driver pulled the long car out into the street.

Jed settled into a seat next to Hathaway. Granny and Elly May were sitting across from them. Jed stretched out his long legs.

"Sure is a lot of room in here," he said to Hathaway.

"Yes, it's quite spacious," Hathaway replied cautiously.

Meanwhile Elly May fiddled with the TV and the CD system. She made the windows go up and down, and then made the sunroof open. She hopped up and stuck her head out.

"Oooowiieee! This sure is fun!" she cried.

"Sit down, Elly May," Granny said, tugging at the young girl's clothes. "Quit jumpin' around like a flea on a griddle."

"But it's fun, Granny," Elly May said.

"I don't care," Granny said. "You know right well you ain't supposed to be standin' up there stickin' yer head out the roof."

"Aw, shucks." Elly May sat down and pouted.

Something started to tweet in the car.

"What's that?" Granny asked.

"Oh, it's just my phone," Hathaway said.

Granny, Jed, and Elly May watched in amazement as Hathaway took the small black phone out of her briefcase and answered it.

"Hello?"

"It's Drysdale, Hathaway. Look behind you."

Hathaway looked out the rear window of the limo. Behind her, Drysdale's white Rolls veered and weaved as Jethro drove it and took in the sights of Hollywood at the same time. Milburn Drysdale was sitting in the passenger seat, struggling hard to stay calm as he spoke on the phone.

"Enjoying the ride, chief?" Hathaway asked.

In the limo Granny watched, bewildered, as Hathaway spoke into the little black thing. "Hey, Jed," she whispered.

"Huh?" Jed looked up.

"She thinks she's talkin' to someone," Granny whispered, pointing at Hathaway. "Here, in the *car*!"

Jed nodded. It did seem mighty peculiar.

"There ain't even no *cord*!" Granny whispered.

"I'll tell him, chief," Hathaway said. Granny nudged her. "Just a minute, chief."

Granny had taken out her flask and was offering it to Hathaway. "Would you like a nip, Miss Hathaway?" she said. "Might make things a little better for ya."

"No, thank you, Granny," Hathaway said, turning to Jed. "Mr. Clampett?"

"That's me," Jed said. He still wasn't used to people calling him Mr. Clampett.

"I have Mr. Drysdale on the phone," she said, holding the phone up.

Granny gave Jed a big wink.

"Mr. Drysdale wants you to know that the bank is ready to help you in any way possible," Hathaway said.

"He said that?" Jed's eyebrows rose.

"I'm sure that's exactly what he just said, dear," Granny said sympathetically, reaching over and patting Hathaway on the knee.

Elly May reached into her pocket, pulled out a wad of chewing tobacco, and bit off a big chaw. Jed watched as the chaw bulged out of her cheek. She rolled down the window and spat.

Jed knew he had to do something about his daughter. Well, he thought, Hathaway had just said the bank was willing to help in any way possible.

"Well, I'll tell you, Miss Hathaway," he said. "There's one reason and one reason only I moved out here. I'm lookin' to get myself hitched."

"Hitched?" Hathaway repeated.

"Sure, you know, hitched," Jed said.

"I'm, er, sorry, but I don't quite understand," Hathaway admitted.

"He's talkin' about gettin' hitched," Elly May said. "Married."

Hathaway's jaw dropped and she quickly pressed her lips to the phone again. "Chief, Mr. Clampett has just mentioned something he'd like to do," she said.

"Fine, anything, just tell me what it is," Drysdale said from the Rolls.

"He'd like to get hitched," Hathaway said into her cellular phone.

Drysdale frowned. "Hitched?"

"Married," Hathaway explained.

"Married?"

"That's what I said, chief."

"Well, Hathaway," Drysdale said. "If J. D. Clampett wants a wife, then you tell him you will personally find him one."

Hathaway could hardly believe her ears. "But, chief, capable as I may be, matrimonial brokering—"

"—is now one of your specialties," Drysdale finished the sentence for her. "Congratulations, and good luck."

"You're serious?" Hathaway asked.

"You have already been fired once today," Drysdale said. "I'd hate to see it happen again."

In the limo Hathaway put away her cellular phone and took out a notepad and pen. "So, Mr. Clampett, what exactly are you looking for in a fiancée?"

"Fiancée?" Jed frowned.

"He ain't lookin' for no fiancée," Granny said. "He's lookin' for a wife."

"Fiancée is French for the person you intend to marry," Hathaway explained.

"How come you're speakin' French all of a sudden?" Granny asked. "That ain't what they speak out in these here Beverly Hills, is it?"

"Well, not everyone does," Hathaway explained. "But some people do."

"We ain't in no foreign country, is we?" Granny said.

Hathaway smiled. "There are people who would claim Beverly Hills is a foreign country."

"Holy smokes, Jed!" Granny gasped. "You heard that? We done moved to a place some people think is a foreign country!"

"Is that true, Miss Hathaway?" Jed asked.

"Not really," Hathaway said. "I was only making a joke."

"A joke?" Granny scowled. "What was so funny about that?"

"Well, maybe it wasn't so funny," Miss Hathaway admitted. "Anyway, we were talking about the kind of woman you wished to marry, Mr. Clampett."

"Well, I'm lookin' for a re-fined lady to help me raise my daughter, Elly May," Jed said.

"Aw, Pa, I'm already raised up," Elly May said, spitting out the window again. "And I'm good and refined, too."

"Don't go spittin' from a movin' car, Elly May." Granny wagged a gnarled finger at her. "You wait for it to stop first, ya hear?"

Jed gave Hathaway a look that said, "See what I mean?"

Hathaway nodded back. The girl was definitely in need of guidance.

The limo pulled through the gates and cruised up the driveway toward the mansion. It stopped in front of the house and the Clampetts and Hathaway got out.

* * *

The limo pulled away down the long driveway. Inside, the driver pulled off his sunglasses
and hat.

Woodrow Tyler smiled to himself as he
steered the limo back out of the estate. He was
going to stay close to these Clampett people.
They were dumb as mules, and the opportunity
to take their money was sure to present itself
soon.

TEN

The next evening Jed strolled through the mansion's foyer while Granny cooked up Sunday supper.

Ding, ding, ding!

A bell rang somewhere. Jed stopped and looked around, wondering where it came from and what it meant.

"Ya-hoo!" Elly May shouted from above. Jed looked up just in time to see her come sliding down the marble staircase banister feetfirst.

"Elly May," Jed said, a tad annoyed, "how many times I got to tell you not to slide down them stairs that way?"

"That way?" Elly May frowned for a moment, then grinned. "Oh, I know what you mean." She ran back up the marble steps.

Ding, ding, ding! There was that darned ringing sound again. Jed looked around, confused. Where was it coming from?

Clunk, clunk, clunk! Now someone was banging on the door. Jed went to the door and opened it. Outside, Milburn Drysdale stood wearing a casual blazer and slacks. With him was a pretty woman wearing a red dress. She was leading that critter with the white pom-poms on a leash.

"Howdy, Mr. Drysdale," Jed said. "Y'all hear some ringing before?"

"Yes, it was the doorbell," Drysdale replied.

"The doorbell?" Jed shook his head in amazement. "Ain't that the dangest thing you ever saw? Every time them bells ring, someone shows up at the door."

"Yes, that is quite amazing," Drysdale said dryly, and turned to his wife. "Don't you think so?"

Margaret Drysdale just stared back at him in disbelief. But Drysdale expected his wife to behave this evening. He'd warned her that the Clampetts were unlike any clients the bank had ever had before. Nonetheless they were the

biggest clients the bank had, and Margaret had better respect that or she was going to start living life without credit cards.

Jed said, "Well, come on in, folks." Milburn Drysdale stepped into the foyer, but his wife hung back, as if she wasn't quite sure what to make of the situation.

"Ya-hoo!" From the top of the stairs Elly May came sliding down headfirst on the other banister. She reached the bottom and did a flip, landing on her feet.

"You were right, Pa!" she cried. "Slidin' down *this* way is a lot more fun!"

"Now, that's not what I meant at all," Jed said. "I didn't want you to slide down neither way. You gots to start actin' like a proper young lady, Elly May."

"Well, I ain't seen it writ nowhere that a proper young lady cain't do some banister slidin' when she feels like it," Elly May said, pouting.

Drysdale stepped back to the doorway and led his wife into the foyer by the arm. "Margaret, dear, please say hello to Jed Clampett and his lovely daughter, Elly May."

"Howdy, ma'am!" Jed shook her hand. "Pleased to meet ya."

"Yeah, same here," Elly May said, shaking Margaret's hand so vigorously that her jewelry jingled up and down her arm.

"Charmed, I'm sure," Margaret muttered.

"So I hopes you brought your appetite with you because Granny's been cookin' up a storm," Jed said.

"I believe Margaret and I are suitably hungry," Drysdale replied, giving his wife a sideways glance.

"Well, good, then," Jed said. "Let's go on into this here other room. Elly May, you know the one I'm talkin' about?"

"I'm not sure, Pa," his daughter replied. "This here house has got so many rooms I still ain't sure I've seen 'em all."

"The one with that big green table," Jed said, "and that big critter's head on the wall."

"Oh, sure," Elly May said. "I know that one. It's where we ate dinner last night."

Jed pushed open a door and held it. Elly May led the Drysdales into a large gaming room. The centerpiece of the room was a magnificent pocket-billiards table, which at the moment had a number of chairs pulled up to it and was set with plates next to each pocket. Beside each chair rested a billiard cue. The rest of the room was lined in dark, burnished mahogany. An immense rhinoceros head hung on one of the walls.

As soon as Margaret saw what they'd done with the billiard table, she turned to her husband and frowned. But Milburn Drysdale shook his head almost imperceptibly, warning his wife not to say anything that might be misconstrued as rude.

"Some table, ain't it?" Jed said proudly.

"I should say," said Drysdale.

"It took me a while a figure out how it worked," Jed said, "but I think I understand how. See, the reason it's set down like that is so's not too many crumbs'll fall on the floor. Likewise, if you spill anything, them little walls'll keep it right there on the table. Now, each of these here little holes is like a small garbage can where you put your bones and claws and such."

"Claws?" Margaret Drysdale repeated.

"Well, sure," said Jed. "Claws, skins, gristle, what have you."

"And just where do these fit in?" Drysdale asked in an amused voice, holding up a cue stick.

Before Jed could answer, the door swung open and Jethro came in carrying two large steaming buckets by their handles.

"Dinner's served," Jed said. "Everybody grab a seat."

The Drysdales watched as Jed, Elly May, and Jethro quickly sat down. Jed picked up his cue stick and slid the tip of it under the handle of one of the steaming buckets. Then he hoisted the bucket toward himself and spooned out the contents with a metal ladle.

He looked up, surprised that the Drysdales were still standing. "Better sit quick," he said. "This here's Granny's best vittles. They'll be gone before you know it."

Drysdale and his wife sat, and he even attempted to lift one of the buckets with his billiard cue.

"I'm tellin' you," Jed said. "It's a mighty interestin' way to eat. Don't reckon we ever saw anything like it back home."

"That's the truth," Jethro said, his cheeks bulging with food.

"I take it you're not aware that you've chosen to have dinner in the billiards room?" Margaret Drysdale asked.

"A billiard, huh?" Jethro said, looking up at the rhinoceros head on the wall. "I was wondering what you called that thing."

Drysdale couldn't help smiling. "No, no, Jethro. This is where you *shoot* billiards."

The door swung open and Granny came in carrying another steaming bucket of food. "Well, you can shoot one, but I ain't gonna cook it. It's too dang big."

"No, no," Drysdale said. "You wouldn't shoot it in here."

"I didn't think so," said Jed. "Be mighty hard to get one of them billiards in here to shoot. You'd be a lot better off shootin' it out in the yard."

"You think there's a season on 'em, Uncle Jed?" Jethro asked. "I was outside all day today and didn't see a single one. And you got to admit, they's pretty hard to miss."

"Well, actually, they're natives of Africa," Drysdale said.

"Who is?" Elly May asked.

"That creature," Drysdale said, pointing at the head on the wall. "You may call it a billiard, but it's actually called a rhinoceros."

"So they're called rhinoceros in Africa," Jed mused. "I still reckon that's an awful long way to go just to get dinner."

The Drysdales looked at each other.

Granny sat down and helped herself to some stew from a bucket. Jed looked around the table. "Well, now that we're all seated here, I'd just like to say that we're mighty glad you folks could come by for Sunday supper."

"Yup, it sure is fortunate for us," Jethro said. "Not only are you folks our neighbors, but you're gonna take care of all of Uncle Jed's money for him."

"Yeah," Granny said with a chuckle. "This way we can keep a close eye on you."

Everyone at the table laughed. Drysdale gestured to the one empty chair at the table.

"Well," he said. "I forgot to tell you that our son, Morgan, was sorry he couldn't join us."

"He had a previous engagement with his friends," Margaret added. To her surprise, Jed took her hand in his and patted it sympathetically.

"Sorry, ma'am," he said. "I imagine that's a real heartbreak. Why, we ain't missed a Sunday supper together since Elly May was born."

"That's right, Jed," said Granny. "The family that eats together keeps together."

They heard a bark and saw Duke come bounding into the room. With their tails wagging happily, he and Babette started to sniff each other.

"I think ol' Duke's sweet on your critter!" Elly May said with delight.

"Babette is not a critter," Margaret replied, pulling the poodle back by the leash. "She's a champion French barbone."

"French, huh?" Jed rubbed his chin thoughtfully. "Seems like there's a lot of French folk around. Why, just yesterday Miss Hathaway was speakin' some French herself."

"I didn't know Miss Hathaway knew French," Drysdale said.

"Well, she asked me if I'd like to marry a French lady," Jed said. "Said I was probably lookin' for one of them there fancies."

"Fancies?" Drysdale scowled.

Meanwhile Elly May was still thinking about dogs. "I've heard of hounds and huntin' dogs and mutts," she said. "But what kind of dog is a barbone?"

"Well, that's simple, Elly May," said Jethro with a grin. "A barbone is a dog that sits outside a bar achewin' on a bone."

"Quite the contrary," said Margaret. "Babette in a purebred standard poodle. Her puppies will be worth three thousand dollars each."

"Three thousand dollars for a dog?" Granny gasped.

"Uh, well, yes, but it's a special situation," Drysdale quickly interrupted. He knew he had to get his wife off the subject of Babette. Perhaps it was best to change the topic of conversation. He turned to Jethro, who was still stuffing his face with food.

"So, son, what do you do?" Drysdale asked.

Jethro pulled a bone out of his mouth and stuck it down the pocket of the billiard table.

"Fine, thanks," Jethro replied.

"No, Jethro," Jed said. "He didn't ask *how* do you do? He asked *what* do you do?"

"What do I do?" Jethro scratched his head with a bone. "Shucks, right now I'm eatin', I guess."

"I meant, what do you do when you're not eating," Drysdale said.

"Well, let's see," Jethro said. "Sometimes I sleep. Sometimes I take ol' Duke for a walk. Sometimes I work on the truck."

"No, I meant, for a living," Drysdale said patiently.

"For a living?" Jethro frowned. "Well, I don't know. What do you do?"

"Me?" Drysdale chuckled and puffed out his chest. "I'm the president of the bank."

"It's a very prestigious and influential position," Margaret added.

"Ooh-wee, that sounds like fun," Jethro said.

"Hey, Uncle Jed, you think I could be president, too?"

"Now, Jethro, that's a mighty disrespectful thing to ask Mr. Drysdale," Jed said. "You don't want to take the man's job. Ask him if you can be *vice*-president."

Suddenly Drysdale deeply regretted ever bringing up the subject. "You? Vice-president? I can't imagine . . . I mean, you're not . . ." He glanced over at Jed, praying the man could talk his nephew out of such an outrageous idea. But Jed just stared back at him with a hopeful grin. Drysdale swallowed.

"Well, we can always use a good man," he said.

"All right!" Jethro grinned. "I'm a vice-president! Now I can get me a fancy office and a pretty secretary!"

Milburn Drysdale pressed his fingers against his eyeballs and instantly regretted what he'd just done.

Ding, ding, ding! The doorbell rang.

Jed looked up. "There goes them bells again," he said. "Jethro, I'll bet there's somebody standin' by that door right now."

"I'll go see." Jethro jumped up and ran out of the room. Drysdale watched him go, wondering what on earth to do with him now that he was a vice-president. When the bank president turned back to the table, he noticed that

Granny had gotten up and was coming toward him.

"I see you two ain't had nothin' to eat yet," she said, picking up a ladleful of stew and pouring it into each of the Drysdales' bowls. "If I's you, I'd eat fast while he's gone."

Margaret looked down into her bowl. It appeared that something with eyes was staring back at her.

"Good Lord, what is it?" she gasped.

"Muskrat fricassee with crushed-cricket stuffing," Granny announced proudly. "And we don't skimp neither. That's the whole muskrat in there."

Milburn Drysdale watched as the blood drained out of his wife's face. The door opened and Jethro returned, followed by Woodrow Tyler, carrying a large bouquet of colorful flowers. Drysdale looked up, aghast.

"Tyler! What are you doing here?"

Woodrow Tyler looked stunned. It was obvious that he had not expected to find his boss there.

"Uh, hello, sir," he said, recovering quickly. "We at the bank took up a collection to buy these wonderful flowers for our newest clients."

He handed the bouquet to Granny. "Welcome to Beverly Hills."

"Why, thank you, sonny," Granny said with a smile.

Drysdale quickly stood up and moved close to his employee. "Can the ham, Tyler," he whispered fiercely. "Introduce yourself and get the hell out of here."

Tyler stepped quickly toward Elly May. "I'm Woodrow Tyler," he said. "I'm very pleased to meet you."

As if to prove that she was a proper young lady, Elly May stood up and offered him her hand to shake. But Tyler, in an attempt to be gracious, bent over to kiss her hand. In one fell swoop, Elly May grabbed him and flipped him over her shoulder.

Thump! Tyler hit the floor on his back and lay there, stunned.

"Elly May Clampett!" Jed gave her a disapproving look.

"Girl, what'd you do that for?" Granny asked.

"Well, he was fixin' to bite my hand," Elly May tried to explain.

"Help him up," Jed ordered.

Elly May picked up Tyler and stuffed him into the empty chair.

Margaret Drysdale turned to her husband and whispered in a horrified tone, "Milburn! These people!"

"Hush, Margaret," Milburn replied, and then turned to Tyler. "I'd apologize if I were you."

"Very well, sir," said Tyler, who was just beginning to recover. "I'm very sorry, Mr.

Clampett. It was really my fault. I, er, moved too quickly. You have a beautiful daughter, and may I say that she's very strong."

"She's too strong for her own good," Granny snapped. "She better change her ways."

Elly May smiled proudly. Jed shook his head wearily and turned to Margaret Drysdale. He had a very important question to ask her.

"Mrs. Drysdale, you see the way my daughter is," he said. "Is there anything we could do to help Elly May become as re-fined as you?"

A number of extremely inappropriate answers raced through Margaret Drysdale's head. Had this hillbilly not been worth one billion dollars, she was certain she would have spoken the truth, which was that Elly May Clampett was clearly beyond help. However, under the present circumstances, that wouldn't be appreciated.

"Well, Mr. Clampett," she said. "I can only tell you what my experience was. I went to finishing school in France."

"What's a finishing school?" Jethro asked.

"If you weren't so danged dumb, you'd know," Granny snapped at him. "It's where you finish school. Now, stop interruptin' the lady."

"I was just going to say that nobody understands refinement and sophistication better than the French," Margaret said.

"Hmmm." Jed rubbed his chin and closed one eye. "I guess what you're really sayin' is we should move ourselves over to France. Is that it, Mrs. Drysdale?"

"Absolutely not!" Milburn Drysdale exclaimed in sudden panic. "You'd hate it in France. You're much better off getting a French tutor to come here."

"What's a tooter?" Elly May asked.

"Now, that's really obvious," Jethro said. "A tooter's someone who blows a horn."

"Guess it would be a French horn if it were a French tooter, huh?" Jed asked.

"Why do I have to learn to blow a horn?" Elly May asked in dismay.

Margaret Drysdale stared at her husband and rolled her eyes as if to say that these Clampett people were utterly hopeless. But Milburn Drysdale was determined to smooth things over.

"Actually, these days French tutors do much more than teach the French horn," he said. "They teach manners and refinement and sophistication. Why, it wouldn't take long at all to change Elly May into the picture of delicate refinement."

"Well, I don't want to change!" Elly May shouted. "I just want to be who I am! And I ain't goin' to no France and I ain't havin' no French tooter come here."

She jumped up and kicked her chair away, then ran from the room.

"Elly May!" Jed jumped up. "Uh, please excuse me, folks." He ran out of the room after her.

A moment of silence descended over the billiard table. Margaret Drysdale noticed that Jethro was staring at the bowl in front of her.

"Excuse me, Mrs. Drysdale," he said. "But if you ain't gonna eat them vittles, can I have them?"

"Most certainly," Margaret Drysdale replied with a sigh of relief. She gingerly slid the bowl toward him, trying her best not to let any of the awful concoction get on her fingers.

She just hoped this would be the last time she'd ever have to visit with these people.

Jed followed a trail of open doors out to the backyard. It was a cool, clear evening and he began to stroll among the gardens and trees. Finally he stopped near a stately cedar tree with long branches that reached down to the ground. Two pairs of eyes glowed at him in the moonlight. Jed made out the silhouettes of two baby raccoons. He knew what must have drawn them there.

"C'mon down, Elly May," he called up into the tree.

His call was greeted with the sound of silence.

"I know you're up there, girl," Jed said, sitting down on the lawn. "Reckon I'll just set myself down here and wait. I got all night, so take your time."

Above him the branches began to rustle as Elly May climbed down a little ways.

"How'd you know where I was, Pa?" Elly May asked.

"Aw, heck, Elly May, it ain't hard to figure," Jed said with a smile. "Ever since you could walk, you been climbin' up trees and cuddlin' with your critters."

Jed took out his whittling knife and started skinning down a piece of cedar. Above him the branches shook some more.

"So what do you want?" Elly May asked from above.

"You know what I want," Jed said. "Elly May, it's high time to think about changin' some things. You should start wearin' dresses and fixin' up nice."

The tree shook some more, and then Elly May dropped to the ground with a soft *thump*. She squatted down next to her father.

"Pa, if I start doin' that, people'll start callin' me a sissy," she complained.

"Naw, Elly May," Jed said. "It ain't sissy for girls to act like girls."

"But I do act like a girl," Elly May insisted.

"Well, I wish it were true, Elly May, but it

ain't," Jed said with a sigh. "See, after your ma died, I did what I knew best to raise you. Trouble was, the only way I knew to raise a young'un was as a boy. So you learned roughhousin', fishin', and fightin'."

"Yeah," Elly May said. "That's fun stuff!"

"I ain't sayin' it ain't," Jed said. "Trouble is, Elly May, nature made you into a girl. And lately she's been gettin' more and more positive about it."

Elly May frowned and looked down at herself. "You mean, with all these bumps and curves 'n stuff?"

"That's what I mean," Jed said. "You don't see too many boys with that sort of stuff. And when you do, you're best off steerin' clear of 'em."

"But it ain't no fair." Elly May sniffed and stared down at the ground.

"Sure, it is." Jed reached over and lifted her chin. "Every time I look into your eyes, I see your ma there."

"Really?"

Jed nodded.

"Tell me about her again, Pa," Elly May begged. "Please?"

"Well, she was real pretty," Jed said. "Just like you."

"Aw, I ain't so pretty," Elly May said with a shrug.

"You sure are," Jed said. "And just like you, your ma had kind eyes and an even kinder heart. Tell you the truth, Elly May, I don't know how I ever fooled someone so beautiful into fallin' in love with an old coot like me."

"Was she refined, Pa?"

"Oh, yeah," Jed said. "She was a real genteel lady. I'll tell you, Elly May. I still miss her so much. Even now."

Jed stared up at the stars and felt a pang in his heart. He was going to be fifty soon. It had been a long time since Katey had passed away. But he still missed her.

Elly May took his hand in hers. "You know what, Pa?" she whispered.

Jed shook his head.

"I want to be just like my ma," Elly May said. "So I reckon I will need somebody to teach me ladylike ways."

"I reckon you do, too," said Jed. "And it's just dumb luck that I got the means to make that happen. So that's what I'm gonna do."

He pushed himself to his feet and helped Elly May up. "Well, we'd better be heading back in before Granny sends out a search party to find us."

"Okay, Pa," Elly May said with a laugh.

Jed slid his arm around her shoulder, and together they walked back toward the big house.

"Child," Jed said affectionately, "I do love to hear you laugh. All your ma and I ever wanted in the world was for you to be happy."

ELEVEN

Early the next morning, when the sky was still gray before the dawn, the creaking sound of a heavily laden wheelbarrow broke the quiet.

"Shoulda brought my piping from back home," Granny muttered to herself as she pushed the wheelbarrow over the dew-laden grass. The wheelbarrow was filled past its brim with copper piping, urns, a silver tea set, bathroom fixtures, and kitchenware Granny had taken from inside the house.

"Now I've got to use these darn knick-knacks," she said to herself. "Well, there's no use in wallerin' about it. The doctors in this holler probably ain't worth swill. There's probably plenty of people in these here Beverly Hills who's ailin' and needs my expert medical treatment."

Finally she reached a spot in the far corner of the estate. Here, in a small grove of trees and shrubs, Granny decided to set up her new still.

A little while later Morgan Drysdale drove his black convertible BMW 325i up the long drive-way and parked in front of the Clampett mansion. Under the threat of being forced to grill frozen cow parts at Burger King, Morgan had agreed to take the woof-woof Clampett daughter, whose ridiculous name was Elly May, under his wing and guide her through her first few weeks of school.

He got out of the car and rang the doorbell, dreading what he was about to see. Suddenly the front door opened and this . . . this amazing *fox* stepped out and shot a big grin at him.

"Howdy," she said. "I'm Elly May. You must be Mr. Drysdale's son."

Morgan was momentarily speechless. *This* was the girl his father wanted him to escort through school? She was incredible—from her authentic blond hair to her big blue eyes to her brilliant smile to the absolutely amazing body stuffed into that tight shirt, jeans, and cowboy boots. Over the shirt she was wearing a denim jacket with a fur collar.

"Well, thanks for pickin' me up," Elly May said. "Is that there your car?"

Morgan couldn't believe it. He felt like he'd just died and gone to heaven. Wait until the guys at school saw her!

Elly May gave him a funny look. "Are we gonna go to school or are you just gonna stand here all day?"

Morgan knew he had to get himself in gear, but somehow he couldn't. Elly May Clampett was too *incredible*!

"Hey, listen," Elly May said. "I'd shut your mouth if I were you. Otherwise some bug's gonna fly in there and make himself a home."

The thought of it snapped Morgan out of his daze. "Right, so let's go."

He went down to the car and held the door open for her. Morgan couldn't remember the last time he'd held a door for a girl.

"It's all right," Elly May said, putting her hand firmly on the door. "I can do it."

"I know you can," Morgan said with a nervous smile. "I was just trying to be polite."

Elly May slammed the door and Morgan got in on the driver's side, and they started off.

"So I forget where my father said you were

Jed Clampett (Jim Varney) watches his property erupt.

Jim Varney as
Jed Clampett.

Granny (Cloris
Leachman)
checks out the
goings-on.

The Clampett clan heads for Beverly . . . Hills that is. From left to right: Jim Varney as Jed Clampett, Erika Eleniak as Elly May, Diedrich Bader as Jethro Bodine, and Cloris Leachman as Granny.

Elly May as played by Erika Eleniak.

Jethro Bodine (Diedrich Bader) having a bit of possum stew.

"Welcome to our new spread." From left: Diedrich Bader as Jethro Bodine, Erika Eleniak as Elly May, Jim Varney as Jed Clampett, Cloris Leachman as Granny, and Lily Tomlin as Miss Jane Hathaway.

Jethrine Bodine
(Diedrich Bader)
in her movie-star
finest.

Miss Jane
Hathaway (Lily
Tomlin) and Mr.
Milburn Drysdale
(Dabney Coleman).

Rob Schneider as
the scheming
Woodrow Tyler.

Granny (Cloris
Leachman)
and Miss Jane
(Lily Tomlin)
act out their
plan.

Miss Jane (Lily Tomlin) and Granny (Cloris Leachman) lead a pack of hillbillies to Jed's rescue.

from," he said as they drove out onto Crestview Drive and toward school.

"Arkansas," Elly May replied, feeling the wind blow in her hair.

"Arkansas, huh? Where exactly is that?"

"Oh, it's half a dozen states over," Elly May said, and pointed off toward the east.

Morgan was certain he'd *heard* of Arkansas. He just couldn't quite picture it in his mind. "So what's it like there?"

"Oh, it's real nice," Elly May said.

"But not like this," Morgan said, gesturing to the rows of tall palms that lined the streets.

"No. We ain't got these kind of trees," Elly May said.

"They're called royal palms," Morgan said, emphasizing the word *royal*.

"Well, they sure are pretty," Elly May said.

Morgan wanted to say, "And so are you," but he didn't.

It wasn't long before they got to Beverly Hills High. Morgan pulled into the parking lot and they passed a long row of beautiful new and shiny BMWs, Porsches, and Mercedes.

"Wow." Elly May gushed. "The teachers here must get paid real good."

"Huh?" Morgan said, caught off guard. "Why do you say that?"

"Well, look at their cars," Elly May said.

Morgan chuckled. "Those aren't the teachers'

cars. Those are the students' cars." He pointed to another lot, where some beat-up-looking Toyotas and Fords were parked. "*That's* the teachers' parking lot."

They parked in the student parking lot and climbed the steps toward the school. Elly May had never seen a school that was so big or so fancy. Even the students looked fancy. They all wore sunglasses and stylish clothes. To Elly May they all looked like movie stars.

Even as they walked up the steps guys and girls started staring at Elly May. Inside the school's corridors, the staring continued. Morgan puffed out his chest and grinned proudly at everyone who looked their way.

"She's with me," he kept saying. "Yup, she's with me."

As they walked down the hall they passed one girl with dyed yellow hair teased out in all directions. She stepped into their path, staring first at Elly May and then at Morgan.

"Hi, Morgan," she said, snapping gum in her teeth. "I see you found a live one."

"Elly May Clampett," Morgan said, "this is Shannon Doherty."

"Pleased to meet you," Elly May said.

"De-lighted." Shannon batted her eyes and imitated Elly May's hillbilly twang. "And by the way, I don't believe in killing animals for their fur."

"Heck, neither do I," Elly May replied. No

sooner were the words out of her mouth than a small animal popped its furry head out of her shirt and snarled at Shannon.

"*Ahhhhh!*" Shannon screamed and jumped away. "It's a rat! She's got a rat."

"It ain't no rat, silly," Elly May said. "It's a ferret." She took the ferret out of her shirt and placed it on the floor. "Okay, Bogey, I think you can find your way home now."

The ferret scurried off, and Elly May and Morgan continued down the hall. Elly May kept saying "howdy" and "hi, y'all" to the students they passed, but the girls mostly ignored her and the guys mostly stared at her body and leered. As they passed a long line of kids waiting to get money from an ATM machine in the hallway, Elly May suddenly stopped and turned to Morgan.

"I don't get it," she said. "I'm tryin' to be friendlylike. But these folks don't seem to want to say 'howdy' back. They sure are shy."

"Who cares about them, Elly May?" Morgan replied. "They're all losers. Not one of them is worth more than three hundred million."

They continued down the hall and passed a small cart, where an attendant in a white uniform was making cups of cappuccino for a group of students. The speakers crackled overhead with an announcement.

"Class will start in five minutes. Please try to arrive before the curtain rises. Also, there's been a change in the lunchroom menu today. The duck-sausage pasta in a light fennel cream sauce is being replaced with blackened mahimahi served over a bed of couscous."

"What was that all about?" Elly May asked.

"Just a change in the lunch menu," Morgan said. "Doesn't matter. The food here sucks, any-way." Suddenly he stopped. "Uh-oh."

"What's wrong?" Elly May asked.

"Trouble," Morgan said, nodding down the hall. Coming toward them were three tough-looking guys wearing hooded sweatshirts and varsity jackets. Morgan took Elly May by the arm and tried to steer her away, but it was too late. They'd been spotted.

"Hey, if it isn't Morgan," said the biggest of the three. His name was Derek. "Spelled big *M*, little organ."

His buddies, Jake and Lance, grinned as Derek grabbed Morgan and got him in a headlock.

"So, Derek, nice to see you." Morgan winced and grimaced as he tried to pull his head out of Derek's grip. "Sorry, but we've got to go."

"Sure, you can go, bank boy," Derek said. "There's just one thing. You gotta cough up your lunch money first."

"Yeah," said Lance. "It's time you con-tributed to the wrestling team's party fund."

"But all I have on me is four hundred dollars in traveler's checks," Morgan pleaded.

"That'll do," said Jake. "Just sign 'em and hand 'em over."

"Not all of it!" Morgan cried.

"Men," Derek ordered, "show Morgan what happened to the last guy who didn't pay up."

Lance walked over to a locker and opened it. A small student was stuffed inside. Lance closed the locker again.

"Look," Morgan said. "I've got an idea. How about I wire the money into your account?"

Derek and the others gave each other questioning looks.

"Okay," Derek said. "But it has to be before the close of business today. Promise?"

"I swear!" Morgan whimpered.

"I'll take possession of your car if you don't," Derek threatened.

"It'll be in your account," Morgan promised. "Don't worry."

Derek let go of Morgan and walked away with his buddies.

Morgan put his hands on his head and swiveled it back and forth as if to loosen it up.

"I don't see why you have to give anything to that big gorilla," Elly May said. "Who does he think he is, anyway?"

"That big gorilla thinks he's the captain of the wrestling team," Morgan said. "And guess what? He is."

"A rasslin' team?" Elly May's eyes went wide.

"Wow, I never rassled a *team* before. Unless you count the McCarter triplets."

"Well, you don't wrestle the whole team," Morgan tried to explain. "What happens is, each person on the team wrestles one person from the opposing team. And at the end, whichever team has won more matches is the winner."

Elly May looked disappointed. "But rasslin' a whole team sounds like fun."

Morgan looked over her voluptuous body again. "Did you, er, wrestle at your old school?"

"Naw, but I did a whole lot of rasslin' outside of school," Elly May said proudly.

"Wow, I guess things are really different in Arkansas," Morgan said. "We don't have women's wrestling teams here. It's strictly for boys."

"Well, back where I come from, everyone rassled everyone," Elly May said. "We rassled girls, boys, bears, you name it."

Morgan started to grin. Now he understood. "You're tryin' to pull my leg," he said.

Elly May frowned. "No, I'm not."

"Yes, you are," Morgan said. "All that stuff about wrestling boys and bears . . . You're just trying to pull my leg."

"Morgan, how can I be tryin' to pull your leg if I'm not even touchin' it?" Elly May asked.

Morgan just laughed. Not only was she great looking, but she had a great sense of humor, too.

*   *   *

Inside the arching marble-and-gold entrance to an expensive spa on Rodeo Drive, Laura Jackson lay on her back, naked except for a towel covering her body from the thighs up. A young beautician wearing a white smock applied hot wax to her legs. The scene would not have been remarkable had it not been for the presence of Woodrow Tyler standing in the corner, pretending to read a *Mademoiselle* magazine while sneaking furtive glances at Laura's magnificent legs.

The beautician kept glancing up at Tyler, obviously flustered by the presence of a man in what was usually a single-sex situation.

"Woodrow," Laura said, slightly annoyed, "don't you have anything better to do today?"

"I just thought you might want to know more about the richest dumb guy in America," Tyler replied. "He's a complete hayseed. A real hillbilly."

The beautician took hold of a strip of cooled wax. *Rippppp!* She yanked it off Laura's leg.

"Gee, honey," Tyler said hungrily. "I don't know why you just don't let me do that."

"So J. D. Clampett's a hillbilly, huh?" Laura said. "That should make it easy, shouldn't it?"

Rippppp!

Tyler watched the beautician work with avid interest. "It doesn't look that hard," he said. "I mean, all you've got to do is get the wax, right?"

Ripppp!

Tyler's interest in her legs was starting to annoy Laura. "Tyler, answer me," she snapped.

"Huh?" Tyler looked up blankly, befuddled by lust.

"I said, our plans for helping J. D. Clampett with his money problems should be *easy*, right?" Laura said.

"Oh, yes, it should be easy," Tyler said. "But we have to weasel our way in soon. Before he gets married."

"Married?" Laura's eyes widened as the beautician spread lotion on her legs. Across the room Tyler opened and closed his hands.

"Now, that, I *know* I can do," he said.

"Don't even think about it," Laura warned him. "Now, what makes you think J. D. Clampett is getting married?"

"Well, he's not," Tyler said. "At least not yet. But he wants to."

Laura could see the whole thing. She knew the kind of woman that was going to go after Clampett. She'd be a shrewd, conniving, money-grubbing, heartless, gold-digging bitch, who would marry him for a few months, then file for divorce and end up with half his money. *Her* kind of girl.

"Is the old goat just horny and looking for some action?" she asked.

"Nah, he just wants a *re-fined* lady to raise his daughter, Elly May," Tyler said, as he watched the beautician pack up her things and leave the room.

"What is she, a kid?" Laura asked.

"Looks to be about sixteen to me," Tyler said.

"And she still needs to be raised?" Laura frowned.

"Yeah, she's a real hellcat," Tyler said. "The other night when I was over there, she flipped me over her shoulder."

"I bet you liked that," Laura said snidely.

"I wouldn't mind it if *you* flipped me over your shoulder," Tyler said.

"So he wants someone to raise his daughter," Laura mused. "What about the mother?"

"I think she must've kicked off just after the girl was born," Tyler said.

"Hmmm." Laura adopted an English accent. "Perhaps Mr. Clampett would like a Mary Poppins–type English governess."

Tyler could picture Laura dressed up like Mary Poppins, with the umbrella. "No, I don't think that's what he's looking for."

"Then maybe a no-nonsense military-type disciplinarian," Laura said.

Now Tyler pictured her in a uniform and holding a riding crop. "Not that either. He seemed to get interested when somebody brought up the idea of a French tutor."

Suddenly Laura smiled. It was very easy to picture herself dressed in chic French clothing—a striped top, tight slit skirt, beret, and most importantly, a diamond the size of the Ritz on her finger.

"Oolala," she said with a French accent. "Are you thinking what I'm thinking?"

"Yeah," Tyler said, staring at her legs again. "I'm thinking how much fun it would be to lock the door, slather ourselves with oil, and pretend we're mud-wrestling."

Laura sighed. This guy had only one thing on his mind. She pressed her lips into a sexy pout. "Come here, baby doll."

Tyler straightened up and looked around. There was no one else in the room, so she must've meant him.

"Me?" he asked, pointing at himself.

"Yes, honey buns, you." Laura sat up on the table and pressed the towel against herself. Then she wagged her finger at him enticingly.

Tyler staggered forward. Could this be it, finally? Here in the spa? He pressed his face up close to Laura's and puckered his lips.

"Ah!" Laura suddenly gasped.

"What's wrong?" Tyler asked.

"Look." Laura held up a small magnifying mirror. Tyler looked at himself and saw several long, ugly nose hairs sticking out of his nostrils.

"Is that a problem?" he asked.

Laura nodded and handed him a waxing

stick. Tyler had watched the beautician use it before. Obviously Laura wanted him to use it on his nose hairs. And once he did, she'd be all his, right there in the spa!

Tyler quickly applied the waxing stick to his nose. Laura waited for it to cool, then grabbed it and yanked.

Rippppp!

"Ahhhhhhhhhhh!" Tyler's scream of pain was heard clear out on Rodeo Drive.

TWELVE

Later that day Jethro was walking through the foyer.

Ding, ding, ding! the doorbell chimed.

Jethro stopped and frowned. Now, what had Uncle Jed said about that bell? Oh, yeah, every time it rang, somebody came to the front door. Jethro quickly pulled the door open, hoping they hadn't gone away.

Standing in the doorway was Laura, wearing a striped shirt, tight slit skirt, and a beret.

"Why, howdy," Jethro said with a big smile.

"Bonjour," Laura said with a French accent. "My name is Laurette Voleur and I am a governess."

"Well, come on inside, ma'am," Jethro said.

Laura stepped into the foyer and looked around, seemingly awed by its vast grandeur.

"So what can I do for ya?" Jethro asked.

"Oh, uh, there is nothing *you* can do for *me*," Laura said. "But there is something I can do for you. I am going door-to-door to see if anyone needs the services of a governess."

She handed Jethro a pink card that read, *From Makeup to Manners, Mademoiselle Laurette Voleur, live-in French governess.* Jethro studied the card intensely for some time before looking up and shaking his head.

"Well, sorry, ma'am," he said. "I don't think we need anyone like you."

"Are you sure?" Laura asked.

"Pretty sure," said Jethro.

"Is there not a young woman in the house who is perhaps a bit unruly?" Laura asked.

Jethro shut one eye and scratched his head. "Not that I can think of, ma'am. But then again, we just moved in here and it's a mighty big house. So I might not have met her yet."

Laura was extremely perplexed. Tyler was right about one thing. These people were so dumb, they didn't even know who they lived with.

An old lady came through the foyer carrying a mop and bucket. She put the bucket down and began mopping the marble floor, but Laura could tell she was listening in on the conversation.

"You are absolutely sure there is no one here in need of refinement and sophistication?" Laura asked.

"Not here," Jethro said. "But you might want to try some of the neighbors."

Just then a man in strange-looking clothes made of animal skins came out on the second floor and started down the stairway to the right. Partway down he suddenly realized his mistake.

"Doggone it," he muttered to himself as he started to back up. "That's the *up* staircase. You got to go down the *down* staircase." He went back up and came down the stairway on the left.

Laura looked up and realized he must be J. D. Clampett himself. She put on her sweetest smile and then turned back to Jethro.

"Well, I am so sorry to have troubled you, monsieur," she said. "I will be going now."

"Now hold on here," Jed said, joining Jethro by the door. "What seems to be the problem, ma'am?"

"I have just come to your door, hoping my services might be needed, but this nice young man said that he didn't think so," Laura said.

"Well, what kind of services do you, er, offer, ma'am?" Jed asked.

152

"I teach, er, how do you say . . . rambunctious teenage girls how to be more ladylike and proper," Laura said, handing Jed her pink card.

"No kiddin'?" Jed said. He took the card and scowled at it.

"Mais oui, monsieur," Laura said. "In fact, I specialize in girls around the age of sixteen who have lost their mothers."

"Well, dog my cats," Jed said. "Mrs. Drysdale was just talkin' about how the French are the best at finishin' a girl out. Ain't that a coincidence?"

"I'll say," Granny muttered to herself as she mopped the floor.

Jethro suddenly brightened. "You know what, Uncle Jed?"

"What, Jethro?"

"I just thought of somethin'," Jethro said excitedly. "Maybe this here French governess could help out with Elly May."

"Why, that's just what I was thinkin', too," Jed said. He turned to Laura. "Now, what'd you say your name was?"

"I am Mademoiselle Laurette Voleur," Laura said.

Jed frowned. "Well, that sure is a mouthful. You wouldn't mind if I just called you Miss Laurette, would you?"

"That would be fine," Laura replied with her warmest smile.

"Well, Miss Laurette, all I can say is this must

be just your day because we got ourselves the exact kind of girl that you say you specialize in."

"Oh, really?" Laura was all excitement. "That is very good news, no?"

"Well, no, I mean, yes, I mean . . ." Jed had gotten sort of tongue-tied. "Tell you what, Miss Laurette. Why don't you just come along and meet her for yourself."

At that moment Elly May was playing in the indoor pool, pushing a raft on which there was a chicken, a cat, an otter, and a duck. Spanky, an orangutan dressed up like a lifeguard, watched from a chair nearby. That sweet boy from next door, Morgan, had arranged for her to have Spanky. He'd told her that his father, Mr. Drysdale the bank president, had told him to do whatever it took to make Elly May happy. Elly May was just delighted. It was hard to imagine that anyone could have nicer neighbors.

Elly May had already given all the animals names. The chicken was named Lamont, the cat, Rascal, the otter, Frankie, and the duck was Elvis. When Jed and Jethro came in with the skinny lady with the tight clothes and the little hat, Elly May told all her animals to behave. That was when Spanky, the orangutan, stuck his tongue out at her.

"You, too, Spanky," Elly May warned.

Jed wasn't surprised to find his daughter soaked to the bone and playin' with a bunch of critters.

"Elly May," he said, "y'all climb out of that cement pond. I want you to meet Miss Laurette here."

"Just a minute, Pa," Elly May said. She turned to her orangutan. "Spanky, it's your job to look out for the others while I'm gone."

Spanky saluted her. Elly May climbed out of the pool. Dripping wet, she offered Laura her hand.

"Howdy, Miss Laurette."

Laura shook her hand. "*Bonjour,* Elly May. It is such a pleasure to meet with you."

"Now, Miss Laurette here is an actual French governess, Elly May," Jed said. "I was thinkin' that every day after school, she could teach you the ways of bein' a lady."

"I thought you was gonna find a wife to do that," Elly May said.

"Well, let's just figure that Miss Laurette can do it until I find me a wife," Jed said.

"But, Pa," Elly May said. "Every day after school I need to go to rasslin' practice."

"Rasslin' practice?" Jed frowned. "You don't need no practice rasslin', Elly May. Why, you're already too good at it."

"Well, Morgan says I cain't be on no rasslin' team if I don't go to the practice," Elly May said,

crossing her arms stubbornly. "An' I wanna rassle, Pa."

A rasslin' team? This was just the kind of problem Jed needed help with.

"Now, Miss Laurette," Jed said. "In your esteemed French opinion, would you say that rasslin' is a ladylike thing to do?"

"I'm afraid not," Laura said. Elly May immediately frowned and looked like she might even cry. Laura noticed that her father also looked very concerned. She quickly realized that Elly May's wanting to be a wrestler was going to be a problem, which could potentially interfere with her employment in the Clampett household.

"What I meant," Laura quickly added, "was that wrestling was not a ladylike thing to do in the past. But now we are in the nineties and many ideas about what is ladylike have changed. So, if it is a sporting situation and in school, it is quite permissible and ladylike to wrestle."

Elly May brightened and a broad smile creased her lips. "Did you hear that, Pa? As long as it's in school and for fun, I can rassle!"

"Now, how about that?" Jed said with a wondrous smile. Laura took his hand and gave him a flirtatious look.

"It is true, Monsieur Clampett," she said. "In this day and age there are things a lady can do that would surprise even a man like you."

Jed scuffed his boot on the ground and

blushed. "Well, I don't doubt that for one second."

"But if I can go to rasslin' practice after school," Elly May said, "I won't have no time for Miss Laurette."

"Nonsense, Elly May," Jed said. "I reckon there'll be plenty of time for both Miss Laurette and rasslin'."

"Ah!" Suddenly Laura felt someone smack her on the butt. She jumped and turned around.

"Aw, don't be scared," Elly May said. "Ol' Spanky here's just showin' you how much he likes you."

Laura took a deep breath and forced a smile on her face. Then she actually reached out and patted the repulsive-looking creature on the head. "Not as much as I like him," she said.

Spanky responded by swatting her on the butt again.

"Oh, you're so naughty!" Laura said with a laugh, wishing all the while she could throw the orangutan in the pool and drown it.

"Well, I guess we just figured out why they call him Spanky!" Jed said with a laugh.

"Tell me," Laura said. "Where did you ever get such a menagerie?"

"Spanky ain't no menagerie," Elly May said. "He's an orang-o-tang."

"Mr. Drysdale's son, Morgan, got him for Elly May," Jed said. "She likes the company. The other critters just kind of showed up on their own. The same way they used to do with Elly May's ma."

"Hey, Jed! Elly May! Miss Laurette!" Jethro shouted. "Come look at this!"

In the room next to the indoor pool was a single bowling alley. Jethro was in there waving at them. The others came over to see what he was up to.

"Uncle Jed," Jethro said excitedly. "I done finally figured out this here game. See, it's a real thinkin' man's game. First you drop the ball down this here slide."

He demonstrated by dropping the ball into the alley. "You see how it starts to roll down yonder?"

Jed and Elly May nodded.

"Now what you do is slide down this here waxed gully," Jethro said. He took a running start and dived onto the alley, sliding headfirst toward the pins.

"Now what you do," he shouted as he slid, "is see how many of them snake-bashin' clubs you can knock down before the ball gets there."

Crash! Jethro smashed headfirst into the pins.

"What an idiot!" Laura couldn't help muttering to herself.

"I'm sorry, Miss Laurette," Jed said. "Did you just say something?"

"Oh, yes," Laura said, returning to her French

accent. "I said that he is obviously a very clever fellow. I assume that he is the brains of the family, no?"

Down at the end of the bowling alley, Jethro sat up and beamed proudly.

Jed, Elly May, and Laura returned to the indoor pool. When they got there, Spanky jumped up and pointed excitedly toward the bowling alley.

"You want to go play with Jethro?" Elly May asked.

Spanky nodded eagerly and jumped up and down, clapping his hands.

"Well, go ahead," Elly May said.

Spanky lumbered over to the bowling alley. Elly May, Jed, and Laura sat down beside the pool.

"Since you an' Elly May are here," Jed said, taking out his whittling knife and a piece of wood. "Why don't you commence with your first lesson."

"Very well," Laura said. "Perhaps we should start with pool etiquette, no?"

"Yes, I mean, no, I mean, whatever . . ." Elly May replied uncertainly.

"Here is the first rule," Laura said. "The pool is for people, not for the critters."

"No critters in the pool?" Elly May frowned.

Before Laura could continue, they were interrupted by Jethro, who was pulling Spanky back

from the bowling alley by the hand. Jethro looked upset.

"You tell him he can't play no more, Elly May," Jethro said.

"Why not?" Elly May asked.

"Because he won't play by the rules," Jethro said. "He keeps wantin' to throw the ball down the alley and have *it* knock down them snake-bashin' clubs. And I keep tellin' him that ain't the way the game's played."

"Now, you listen to me, Spanky," Elly May said, wagging a scolding finger at the ape. "If you play the game the way Jethro wants to, maybe later Jethro will play the game the way you want to."

"Now, that seems fair, don't it?" Jethro asked Spanky.

Spanky just shrugged and nodded, and headed back toward the bowling alley.

"So where were we?" Elly May asked, turning back to Laura.

"I am trying to say this," Laura said. "The people go in the pool, and the chickens go in the coop. We do not want chicken poop in the pool. We want the chicken poop in the coop."

"Now, you listen to her, Elly May," Jed said, looking up from his whittling. "Miss Laurette, you sure do make everything sound downright poetic."

Laura gave him her absolutely sweetest smile.

"Why, thank you, Monsieur Clampett. You are very kind."

Jed smiled back and blushed a little. "Aw, heck," he said. "It weren't nothin'."

At this moment Granny came in with Miss Hathaway, who had just driven up the driveway and past the herd of cattle Jed had purchased to keep the front lawn grazed. Granny carried a yellow plastic laundry basket piled high with laundry, and Hathaway was clutching a folder of papers tightly to her bosom.

Granny stopped, put down the laundry, and pulled out her flask. "Want some medicine, Miss Hathaway? You seem a might high-strung today."

"No, thank you, Granny," Hathaway replied.

Granny took a pull from the flask, and then closed it up and picked up the laundry again.

"Do you take that everywhere?" Hathaway asked.

"Don't never leave home without it," Granny replied with a wink. She walked past the pool to the hot tub and dumped the basket of dirty laundry in. Then she stepped over to the control panel and turned the whirlpool on. Immediately the water erupted and a whirring sound filled the air.

"This sure is a modern advancement in clothes washing," Granny said as she sprinkled in a small amount of laundry soap. The churning water was soon covered by a thick layer of foam.

Granny pulled an old metal washboard out of the bottom of the laundry basket, then knelt beside the hot tub and began scrubbing the clothes.

"This here contraption practically washes the clothes for ya," Granny said as Hathaway watched in amazement. "Keeps the water hot so you don't have to add water from the fire. The only thing I cain't quite figure is why they'd put it here in the room with the concrete pond. Unless that's where you're supposed to rinse 'em. What do you think, Miss Hathaway?"

"Well, I think you should use the house any way you see fit," Hathaway replied diplomatically.

"Well, all's I kin say is if that concrete pond is where they used to rinse their clothes, the family who lived here before us must've had a whole lot of laundry."

From the side of the pool came the sound of laughter. Granny and Hathaway looked over at where Jed was standing with Elly May and Laura.

"Thar's that new tooter Jed done hired for Elly May," Granny whispered. "She's a ferener, and I ain't sure I trust her."

"Oh, come now, Granny," Hathaway said. "There's no reason to mistrust foreigners in this day and age. We all live in a global village."

"That's just what I mean!" Granny hissed. "We all live in the village and *she's* from out of town."

It was difficult to argue with that kind of

logic. Hathaway thought it would be polite to go over and greet the new tutor.

"Greetings, Mr. Clampett," she said as she joined them.

"Howdy, Miss Hathaway," Jed said, getting up. "Elly May's gettin' her first etiquette lesson from Miss Laurette. She's a governess from France."

"From France?" Hathaway smiled. "How wonderful! *Bonjour, Mademoiselle Laurette. Comment allez-vous?*"

"Tut, tut." Laura wagged a finger at her. "I must only speak English in front of Elly May. Do you not agree, Monsieur Clampett?"

"If that's what you think, Miss Laurette," Jed replied.

Crash! In the bowling alley, Jethro smashed headfirst into the pins again. Laura could hardly believe her eyes. Meanwhile Hathaway stood next to Jed and opened the file she'd brought.

"I've drawn a list from the Bank of Commerce clientele, Mr. Clampett," she said. "Here are the preliminary bridal prospects for you."

Laura heard this and watched as Hathaway lifted out several photographs. This could be a problem, she thought.

"Now, Elly May," she said. "Let us take the chicken back to the chicken coop."

Laura hated animals, but she bent down and

picked up the awful creature anyway. As she walked past Hathaway she allowed the squirming bird to make an escape attempt. In trying to catch it, she "accidentally" knocked the folder out of Hathaway's hands and into the pool.

"Oh, no!" Hathaway shrieked as the papers and photographs settled onto the surface of the water.

"Mon Dieu!" Laura pressed her hands to her cheeks. "How clumsy of me! I am so sorry."

Hathaway ran to the side of the pool, picked up the pool net, and fished the papers out. But it was no use. They were completely waterlogged and tore when she tried to pick them up.

"I'll have to go to the bank and get a duplicate set," she said sadly. "But don't worry, I shall return."

Now Jethro came over from the bowling alley. He'd had a lot of fun playing against Spanky, even though the orangutan wouldn't play by the rules and insisted on throwing the ball down the alley to knock down the snake-bashing clubs. Jethro, on the other hand, had insisted on using his head until the very end. But, unfortunately, it had started to hurt.

"You goin', Miss Hathaway?" he asked.

"Yes, I must return to the bank," she said.

"But you just got here." Jethro looked disappointed.

It appeared that he actually liked her com-

pany. Hathaway was sincerely touched. "I'm sorry, Jethro," she said regretfully, "but business calls."

"All right, then, how's about I walk you to the door?" Jethro asked.

"Why, that would be delightful," Hathaway said with a smile.

Jethro and Hathaway headed toward the front while Laura and Elly May carried the chicken out to the back. Jed watched his daughter and her new tutor leave.

"That thar tooter seems like a real nice gal," Jed said. "I'm glad Elly May's finally gettin' some female company."

"I don't know, Jed," Granny muttered, shaking her head.

"Well, the important thing's that Elly May kind of takes to her, Granny."

"Maybe, but I still don't trust her," Granny said. "She's too darn skinny. She gotta stand in the same place twice before she can cast a shadow."

"Well, maybe you can help her out, Granny," Jed said. "Now that she's gonna be livin' here, you could take it upon yourself to fatten her up."

Meanwhile Jethro walked Hathaway out to her sports car.

"That sure is a nice little car you got there, Miss Hathaway," Jethro said.

"Do you like it?" Hathaway smiled. "Perhaps we could go for a drive someday."

"That'd sure be nice," Jethro said, opening the door for her.

"Why, thank you, Jethro," Hathaway said as she got into the car. It had been a long time since a man had held a door for her and acted so politely. And he was awfully handsome, she thought. So what if he wasn't that bright? Brains weren't *everything*.

Jethro closed the Miata's door, but kept his hand on it. "You know, Miss Hathaway, I was wonderin' if I could ask you a question."

"Of course," she said. "Ask anything. I want you to think of me as being at your service."

"Well, it's about this new job at the bank," Jethro said. "You reckon I can do it? I mean, I've never been a vice-president." He leaned closer to the car. "Tell you the truth, Miss Hathaway, I ain't never even been in a bank."

"I don't think you should worry, Jethro," Hathaway said. "Just buy yourself a nice suit and you'll be fine."

"You mean, all you need to be a banker is a nice suit?" Jethro asked, surprised.

"Right," Hathaway replied. "That's ninety percent of the job right there."

Jethro grinned. "Well, thanks for the advice."

"Anytime, Jethro." Hathaway smiled and started her car. It was wonderful knowing a man who was both polite and valued your opinion.

"Bye, now." She waved.

"Bye-bye, Miss Hathaway." Jethro waved back. "Guess I'll be seein' you at the bank before long."

Hathaway drove back down the driveway. She was so pleased that she actually changed her car radio from the classical station she always listened to, to one that played country music. As she approached the gate she saw that a rather large cow had wandered away from the herd and was standing in the middle of the driveway, blocking her path.

She stopped and beeped her horn, but the large creature paid no attention. Oh, darn, what was she going to do now? Then she remembered the intercom at the gate. She got out of the car and managed to squeeze around the beast, and just barely reached the intercom button.

"Hello? Can anyone hear me?" she yelled, pressing the button.

Back in the mansion, Jethro was standing in the foyer when he heard Hathaway's voice. It sounded like she was real close, but he knew that wasn't possible because he'd just seen her drive away.

"Please, can somebody help me?"

There it was again! Jethro couldn't believe it. Miss Hathaway must've turned around and come back to the house. But where was she?

"Hello? Hello?"

Doggone! It seemed like her voice was coming from inside the wall. "I can hear you," Jethro said. "But where are you?"

Outside, Hathaway hadn't heard anything Jethro said because he hadn't pushed the intercom button. She looked around despairingly at the long wall that surrounded the house, and then spoke into the intercom once more.

"Can someone let me out of here? I'm trapped inside the walls!"

Jethro stared at the walls in disbelief. Trapped inside them? Why, he'd never heard of such a thing! Still, he couldn't just let her stay in there.

"Stay put, Miss Hathaway!" he shouted. "I'll get you out!"

He looked around and spied a large brass coatrack. That would have to do. Picking it up, he swung it at the wall like a baseball bat.

Crash! Plaster dust filled the air and pictures fell off the walls. Jethro stuck his head in the hole he'd just made.

"Miss Hathaway!" he shouted. "Where are you?"

THIRTEEN

It was morning. Before starting her tutorial session with Elly May, Laura luxuriated in a massive marble bathtub in the ornate bathroom attached to her suite. She soaked in a bubble bath, sipped expensive French champagne from a fluted glass, and now and then plucked a bonbon from a silver candy dish as she read a magazine article about Swiss banks. Everything was going better than planned. Her only real concern was that

that idiot Hathaway might somehow find a wife for *Monsieur* Clampett. She'd given the job of making sure that didn't happen, to another idiot whose name was Tyler.

She picked up her cellular phone and called him.

The phone rang in the bungalow, where Tyler—wearing only a shirt, tie, and boxer shorts—sat on the edge of the bed, watching Laura's "Buns of Steel" tape while he got dressed for work. An open pizza box lay on the floor beside him, and he held a slice of last night's pizza in one hand and a warm can of Shasta orange soda in the other. It wasn't quite heaven in his mind. Were he in heaven, he would have been drinking an Orange Crush.

Tyler picked up the phone. "Hello?"

"Hello, Tyler," Laura said. She knew instantly that he was watching the "Buns of Steel" tape. She could hear the music over the phone.

"Oh, hi, Laura. Where are you?" Tyler asked, somewhat distracted by the flexing derrieres on the TV screen.

"I'm in the Clampett mansion," Laura snapped. "Where did you think I was?"

"Oh, yeah, right. I forgot."

Laura took another sip of champagne. "Anyway, this is going to be easier than I thought. First comes love, then comes marriage, then comes a billion in a baby carriage."

"So they're buying the French thing?" Tyler asked.

"Mais oui, certainement!" Laura chirped. "They're total bumpkins. It's a crime they have so much money. It's worse than an illegal alien winning the lottery."

"So we're right to take it away from them," Tyler said.

"Absolutely."

"Oh, yeah. Oh, yeah!" Tyler couldn't help groaning. On the TV was a great rear-end shot of the girls doing donkey kicks.

Laura was getting annoyed by his breathless groans. "Tyler, what are you doing?"

"Oh, uh, I'm just watching the news," Tyler said. He grabbed the remote control to lower the volume, but he hit the up button instead.

"Concentrate on how beautiful your buns are going to be. . . ." The narrator's voice on the tape blared before Tyler could get the volume back down.

"Let me guess," Laura quipped. "They're doing a story about baking your own hamburger buns."

"Hey, it's lonely here without you," Tyler said with a sniff.

"Well, listen to my plan," Laura said. "I know exactly what I'm going to do. First, I'm going to get J. D. Clampett hooked."

"How?" Tyler asked.

"Easy," Laura said with confidence. She raised one of her long, slender legs out of the bathtub and smoothed off the bubbles with her hand. "I can make any man want me. Next, I'll put a little window dressing on Elly May and let her father think I've turned her into a real lady. Then, when the time is right, I'll play one off the other. Believe me, Woodrow, they won't know what hit them."

Tyler raised his hairy leg off the bed and scratched it. "Hey, you're not going to sleep with him, are you?"

"That's not your problem," Laura replied. "Your problem is keeping Hathaway from getting suspicious."

"Well, she's been working night and day trying to find a wife for the old hillbilly."

"Well, you better make sure that doesn't happen," Laura said.

On the TV the camera angle turned to a front shot of the sexy women doing donkey kicks. Tyler was beside himself. "Hey, Laura," he panted, "pretend I've got my hand on—"

A tone blipped over the phone. It was call waiting.

"Hold on a second," Tyler said. "I've got someone on the other line."

He clicked the phone. "Hello? Hello?" No one was there, so he clicked again.

"Okay," he said. "Now I've got my hand on your butt and I'm squeezing."

"Ahem." Someone on the line cleared his throat. "Tyler?"

"Mr. Drysdale!" Tyler practically choked.

"Please get your hand off my butt, Tyler," the bank president snapped.

"Yes, sir." Tyler wondered why Drysdale was calling him before work. He'd never done that before. It must be important.

"I have a very important task for you to do before you come to work this morning," Drysdale said.

"Yes, sir. Absolutely. If it's important, I'm your man."

"There's a pastry shop over on your end of town that Margaret likes," the bank president said. "Stop in there on your way to work and pick up a pound of French pastries. Margaret and I are having company tonight."

"Uh, right," Tyler said, writing it down on the pizza box. "And may I suggest a baguette while I'm there?"

"Excellent idea," Drysdale said. "See you at the office."

Tyler hung up and smiled to himself. His suggestion was a true stroke of genius. That little extra effort would pay off someday. He could just see himself as a vice-president.

A little while later someone even more unlikely saw himself as a vice-president. His name was Jethro Bodine, and in case he forgot it,

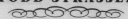
there was a large wooden nameplate on his desk to remind him. Wearing a brand-new suit and tie, Jethro sat in his new office, pressing a pencil into an electric pencil sharpener. With a high-pitched whir, the little machine ground the pencil clear down to the eraser.

Jethro added the eraser to the small pile on his desk and pulled open his drawer to find another pencil. Darn, he was all out.

"Excuse me, Miss Tracy?" he called to his new secretary.

An attractive, young blonde in a tight dress and high spiked heels stuck her head in the doorway. "Yes, Mr. Bodine?"

"I done run out of pencils," Jethro said.

"Here's another box, sir." Tracy teetered toward him on her high heels and handed him a box. As she was leaving, Hathaway entered the office. The look she gave the sexy, blond secretary was not a kind one. Then she turned to Jethro and smiled.

"Hello, Jethro."

"Howdy, Miss Hathaway." Jethro grinned at her.

"My, you look strapping in your new suit," Hathaway said. "Is it Armani?"

"Nope, I'm pretty sure it's wool," Jethro said, scratching himself. "It sure does itch like wool."

"You've got quite a sense of humor," Hathaway said with a smile.

"Why, thanks," Jethro said.

"So, I sent two workmen over to the house this morning to fix that hole in the wall," Hathaway said. "It was very chivalrous of you to try and save me."

"Except you weren't in there," Jethro said sheepishly.

"Well, look at the bright side," Hathaway said. "Now you know how an intercom works."

"I do?" Jethro wasn't sure what she was talking about, but he decided not to pursue it further. He started to open his new box of pencils, then got an idea.

"Uh, Miss Hathaway?"

Hathaway leaned on his desk and gave him her most charming smile. "We're colleagues, Jethro. Call me Jane. Me Jane, you Jethro."

"Well, okay, Miss Jane," Jethro said. "Can I ask you something?"

"Ask away!" Hathaway said gaily.

Jethro took a new pencil out of the box and pressed it into the electric pencil sharpener, grinding it right down.

"Do you think you could get me one of these here electronic whittlers for Uncle Jed?" Jethro asked. "It's his birthday soon. He's gonna be fifty."

"Not a problem," Hathaway said. "And I'll tell the chief about your uncle's birthday. I'm sure he'll want to mark the occasion with an appropriate affair."

"That sounds nice, Miss Jane," Jethro said. "But I was thinkin' he might like a party more."

"Right." Hathaway nodded. "Speaking of your uncle Jed, I should go back to the job at hand."

Jethro's jaw dropped. "You serious?"

Hathaway frowned. "Why, what did I say?"

"You're gonna quit the bank?"

"Did I say that?" Hathaway asked, surprised.

"Well, you said you were gonna go back to the job at hand," Jethro said. "And this here ain't hand. This here's the Bank of Commerce."

"Oh, yes," Hathaway said, laughing. "I'm not leaving the bank, Jethro. That was just a matter of speech. What I meant was, I should go back to the job of finding him a suitable wife."

"Even if she don't wear a suit all the time," Jethro added.

"Uh, right," Hathaway agreed.

"You know," said Jethro, "maybe I could help. Heck, back in the holler my ma was known as the best matchmaker around."

"Is that so?" Hathaway asked.

"Yup." But then Jethro scowled. "I'm just tryin' to remember exactly how she did it."

Jethro was hunched over and so deep in thought that Hathaway couldn't resist getting up to massage his neck.

"Maybe this will help loosen up those memories," she cooed.

"Hmmm." Jethro leaned back and enjoyed her comforting hands. "Yep, I think it's coming back."

"Oh, do tell," Hathaway said.

"Well, the first thing my mama would do was get the back-fence gossips to start jawin'."

"We could drop a few items in the trades," Hathaway mused.

"And then she'd hang a sign on the church bulletin board," Jethro said. "Maybe we should rent us a big bulletin board."

"Well, for a man of your uncle's stature, I think we might want to be a little more discreet," Hathaway said. "Tell me, Jethro, what are your uncle's favorite things?"

"Shoot, that's easy," Jethro said. "Uncle Jed likes smoked crawdads, sow belly 'n hand-slung chitlins, and sponge cake."

The thought left Hathaway slightly queasy. She finished massaging Jethro's neck and moved around to the front of the desk. "Uh, besides food, what does he like?"

"Well, let's see." Jethro rubbed his chin and cocked one eye toward the ceiling. "I guess he likes folks that never waste anything. . . ."

"Go on," Hathaway said with a nod.

"Uh, his favorite song is 'Your Cheatin' Heart' by Hank Williams."

Hathaway sighed. None of this would help her find the right woman for J. D. Clampett.

Little did Jethro or Hathaway know that someone was eavesdropping on their conversation. At his desk out in the main office Woodrow Tyler bent his head down, listening carefully on his intercom to everything Jethro had said. Unlike Hathaway, Tyler had already found the right woman for J. D. Clampett. Now it was simply a matter of putting out the bait and reeling in the fish.

The following day Jed was sitting out on the terrace, whittling. It wasn't exactly the most peaceful morning. Jethro had done bought himself some sort of motorcycle called a dirt bike and was ridin' all over the yard, makin' one heck of a racket. But in a moment of silence, Jed thought he heard the strains of familiar music wafting out the window. He stopped whittling and cocked his head. Could it be? Well, doggone, it was!

He stood up and walked back into the house, following the music to its source. Finally he came to Miss Laurette's room. The door was open, but being a polite man, Jed knocked first.

Inside, Laura was sitting on her bed, pretending to sew up a tear in an old dress. She looked up and pretended to be surprised to see Jed by the door.

"*Entrez,*" she said.

"That means *come in*?" Jed asked.

Laura nodded and smiled as Jed stepped into the room and stood by the door.

"Well, excuse me for interruptin' your sewin', Miss Laurette," he said, "but would that be Hank Williams I hear?"

Laura brought her hand to her mouth and gasped. "Oh, dear! I am so sorry. It must be too loud."

"You cain't play 'Your Cheatin' Heart' too loud for me," Jed said. "I didn't know they listened to him over in France."

"Oh, yes, Hank Williams is very popular in France," Laura said. "I always listen to him while I'm mending an old dress. You know what they say. Waste not, want not."

"One of my favorite sayin's," Jed said.

"But I will have to stop soon," said Laura, "because my sponge cake will be ready."

"You cookin' up a sponge cake?" Jed's eyebrows rose.

"Oh, yes. Sponge cake is my specialty," Laura said. She began to sway to the music. "I love this music. It makes me want to dance."

The next thing Jed knew, Miss Laurette stood up and stepped close to him. She took his hand and they began to waltz around the room. At just the right moment she pressed her face close to his.

"You are a wonderful dancer, Monsieur Clampett," she said softly. "And a very attractive man."

"Why, thank you, ma'am," Jed replied.

"Whomever Miss Hathaway finds for you to marry is going to be very happy," Laura said. "And all women know that happiness is hard to find."

"Pardon?" Jed didn't quite follow.

"Happiness," Laura repeated in a whisper, moving even closer.

It had been a long time since Jed had been this close to a woman. It not only made him nervous, but made him think of Katey, too. He abruptly pulled away. "Yes, well, I guess I done disturbed your work enough, ma'am."

Laura was surprised that he'd been able to resist her. Now she noticed the smell of smoke coming through the doorway. *"Zoot alors!"* she cried. "I smell smoke. I hope it is not my sponge cake."

Laura ran out of the room followed by Jed. The trail of smoke grew thicker and stronger as they went down the hall, through the master bedroom, and into the master bath. There, thick smoke seeped out from around a glass door lined in cedar. Laura found herself staring into a small, smoky room. Inside, hams and large slabs of bacon hung on a clothesline.

"My God," she said. "What is this?"

"Kind a convenient, ain't it?" Jed asked, proudly hooking his thumbs under his suspenders. "An indoor smokehouse."

Laura blinked and reminded herself to use her French accent. "But Monsieur Clampett, this is a sauna. It is not for ham and bacon. It is for people."

"People?" Jed frowned.

"And people only," Laura said.

"You mean, they got cannibals in these here Beverly Hills?"

Laura couldn't tell if he was serious or not. No one could be *that* stupid, could they? Playing it safe, she just smiled sweetly. "Oh, you silly hillbilly."

Jed smiled back, although he wasn't certain what Laurette found so amusing.

FOURTEEN

Jethro had been busy. He respected the job Miss Jane was doing to find Uncle Jed a wife, but he didn't quite grasp why it was so important to be discreet about it. So he'd taken a few steps of his own.

Now it was night and he was out in the truck with Hathaway. They were driving down a road called Sunset Boulevard, and the truck was coughing and backfiring as usual. People

on the sidewalk kept turning and pointing at them.

"Jethro, have you considered getting a new car?" Hathaway asked.

"No, but I told Uncle Jed we should slap a new coat of paint on this one," Jethro replied.

"Well, that would be a slight improvement," Hathaway allowed.

"That's what I thought," said Jethro. "But you know Uncle Jed. He said just because we had money, we didn't need to go showin' off."

Hathaway had to smile to herself. You could take the hillbilly out of the hollow . . . but you couldn't take the hollow out of the hillbilly.

"Well, I just thought you would look wonderful in a big, new, flashy car," Hathaway said. And she could picture herself seated beside him. The thought made her giddy. She took a lipstick out of her purse and applied it to her lips.

Jethro turned to her and grinned. "You sure did get yourself all prettied up this evening, Miss Jane."

"Why, thank you, Jethro." She batted her eyes at him. It was oh so wonderful to have the attentions of a handsome man.

Jethro glanced ahead and saw something. "Okay, Miss Jane, I'm just about ready to pull over. Close your eyes."

The implications thrilled Hathaway. It had been ages since a boy had wanted to kiss her.

And in a car! She slid closer to Jethro in the car seat and shut her eyes tight. "You're so impulsive, you romantic devil."

"Hot diggity dog!" Jethro was filled with excitement. "Okay, now just keep those eyes closed."

"How charmingly old-fashioned," Hathaway said with a wistful sigh. She felt a thrill race through her and shut her eyes. She puckered her lips and waited. She felt the car swerve to the curb and stop. How exciting! How risqué! Right there, at the curb on Sunset Boulevard! Like a couple of impatient teenagers!

"Okay . . ." Jethro moved close to her.

Hathaway caught her breath. Here it came!

"Open your eyes!" Jethro yelled.

Huh? That wasn't what was supposed to happen. Hathaway opened her eyes. It took a moment to focus, and then she found herself staring up at an enormous billboard lit with bright lights. There on the billboard was a huge blowup of Jed Clampett puffing on a corncob pipe! And printed in big letters beneath it, for all of Los Angeles to see was

BILLIONAIRE NEEDS WIFE.
PLEASE CALL 1-800-WED-JED

"Ohmygod!" Hathaway gasped.

"Ain't it somethin'?" Jethro beamed.

"Ohmygod," Hathaway gasped again.

"I know." Jethro nodded. "I felt the same way. Who would've thought old Uncle Jed could look that good?" He leaned close to the stunned Hathaway. "Tell you the truth, Miss Jane, I think them fellers at the billboard company done fixed him up some."

"The chief's going to kill me," Hathaway groaned.

"What?" Jethro frowned.

"I said, Mr. Drysdale is going to kill me."

"You mean, 'cause you didn't think of it first?" Jethro asked. "Aw, heck, Miss Jane, I don't care. You can go and tell him it was all your idea."

Jane Hathaway just stared at Jethro. He was a dear, sweet boy, but such an idiot!

It was late, and as was his habit, Milburn Drysdale was settling down in the den with a sandwich and a glass of milk to watch the local news. He flicked on the set and caught the credits of some TV movie. He knew a block of commercials would come on, followed by the news. Uninterested in the commercials, he looked down at the TV section to see what was on *Nightline* that night.

"Ladies, are you looking for the perfect husband? Then consider Jed Clampett," someone on the TV said.

Drysdale had just taken a sip of his milk when he heard that. Looking up, he found himself staring into the face of a nervous-looking Jethro Bodine, who was on the TV screen.

Blech! The milk flew out of Milburn's mouth. There was no mistake. There was Jethro, wearing a ridiculous bow tie, looking stiff as he recited his lines. Jethro held up a photo of Jed.

"Yes, ma'am, Jed Clampett is rated triple *A*. *A* for attractive. *A* for available. And *A* for a billionaire. So come on down to the Commerce Bank of Beverly Hills and see me, Jethro Bodine, Vice-President."

"No!" Milburn felt the wind go out of him. The half-finished glass of milk fell to the floor with a crash. He was ruined. Absolutely ruined. The board of directors would have his head!

Meanwhile Jethro wasn't finished. "And remember, I'm not only Jed Clampett's wife finder. I'm also his nephew."

"Lord have mercy!" Milburn Drysdale muttered.

When Drysdale got to work the next morning, the line of women who wanted to be Jed Clampett's wife stretched from the front of the bank, down the steps, and around the block. There were hundreds of them! They came in all shapes and sizes.

Milburn Drysdale was appalled. Someone had

to be held accountable for this travesty, and it sure as hell wasn't going to be him!

He limped into the building. Ever since he'd seen that inane advertisement last night, his back had been acting up. The line of women went down a hall, up a flight of stairs, and down another hall to Jethro Bodine's office.

Inside, Hathaway was sitting at a desk, taking information from a tall redheaded woman.

"All right, Miss Jones, here's your number," Hathaway said, handing the woman a white card with a number printed on it. "Please stand over there and have your picture taken. And hold the card beneath your chin so that the number appears in the photo."

The woman stepped over to the other side of the office, where Jethro snapped a Polaroid photo of her. Drysdale felt his blood begin to boil.

"Hathaway!" he shouted.

Caught by surprise, Hathaway jumped. The pen she'd been using flew out of her hand. "Yes, chief?"

"What's going on here?" Drysdale shouted, flying into a rage. "Do you realize you're embarrassing this institution? This is a carnival! A sideshow! Is this a result of that stupid commercial? What kind of numbskull would think up a hare-brained scheme like this?"

"That'd be me, Mr. Drysdale," Jethro said proudly.

"You?" Drysdale swallowed. The pain in his back suddenly got worse.

"That's right." Jethro grinned.

"Why, it's . . . it's brilliant! Insightful! Cutting edge!" Drysdale slapped Jethro on the shoulder. "You're a born leader, son."

Hathaway cleared her throat. "I reckon . . . er, I mean, we've had one thousand two hundred and fifteen women respond to the ad." She thumbed through the photos. "And two men. Once I've entered the data into the computer and done my magic . . . presto! Then we'll narrow them down to a precious few."

"Yes, presto," Drysdale said weakly. Then he leaned close to Hathaway. "But you're not validating their parking tickets, are you?"

"You'll be pleased to know that we are," Hathaway replied.

"That was my idea, too," Jethro said.

Drysdale forced a grin on his face and whipped out a pocket calculator. "Good, good idea. Let's see. That's one thousand two hundred and fifteen women . . . and two men, at one-fifty every fifteen minutes. Ah, there, I'm sure it won't cost me more than five thousand dollars. Hathaway, call my chiropractor."

Rubbing his back, he staggered out of the office.

* * *

Elly May had been pestering Morgan about the wrestling team for days. Finally he gave in.

"I'm telling you, Elly May, this is a bad idea," he said. "No girl has ever joined the wrestling team here. In fact, I called a friend of my dad's who works on the *L.A. Times,* and he said, as far as he knew, no girl in the entire country has ever wrestled on a boys' team."

"Well, Miss Laurette said I could do it, so I'm gonna," Elly May said stubbornly.

They got to the gym and stopped in the doorway. Inside, Derek, the big guy who'd hassled Morgan a few days before, was wrestling someone. Derek picked up the other wrestler and slammed him to the matt, then pinned him.

Some other wrestlers watching from the sides of the mat hooted and hollered. Derek jumped up and danced triumphantly around his opponent.

The team coach, a balding man reading *Variety,* looked up from the paper and blew his whistle. "Okay, boys, practice is over. Hit the sauna and don't harass the masseuse."

"The gym, slash, health club," Morgan whispered to Elly May.

"Well, come on, Morgan, let's go in," Elly May said.

But at the sight of Derek and his buddies, Morgan froze, reluctant to expose himself to more abuse.

"Come on, Morgan." Elly May tugged at his shirt, and Morgan stepped into the gym.

Derek and his buddies spotted him.

"Hey, Organ," Derek said with a malicious grin. "What are you doing here? You come to wrestle me?"

"Well, no," Morgan stammered. "I was just—"

"I know," Derek said brightly. "You came to kiss the gym floor."

Before Morgan could protest, Derek grabbed him in a hammerlock and pressed his face to the floor.

"Kiss it! Kiss it!" Derek's buddies, Jake and Lance, chanted.

Morgan kissed the gym floor. Elly May hated to see her friend humiliated like that. She stepped up to Derek.

"Why don't you pick on someone your own size?" she asked.

Derek let go of Morgan and turned to face her. Elly May noticed that the other wrestlers had come over to see what was going on.

"What business is it of yours, baby?" Derek asked.

"I ain't no baby," Elly May insisted. "I'm all growed up."

"I'll say you are," Derek said with a leer. The other wrestlers hooted and laughed.

"That was a good one, Derek!" Jake cheered.

Meanwhile Derek still had his eyes on the

more developed aspects of Elly May's anatomy. "Maybe you came by to join the wrestling team," he said.

"As a matter of fact, that's right," Elly May said. Morgan staggered to his feet and stood behind her.

"Yeah!" "All right!" "Way to go!" the other wrestlers shouted.

"Hey, man," Lance said with a big grin, "I've got a few holds I'd like to show her."

"I don't wrestle girls," Derek said. "At least not in the gym."

"We know!" "We know!" the others shouted.

"But," Derek continued, "in your case, I'd be glad to make an exception."

"Good!" Elly May said, and gave him a quick push.

Caught off guard, Derek tumbled backward. A couple of the other wrestlers chuckled.

"Hey, Derek, you gonna let a girl push you around?" one asked with a laugh.

Derek scrambled to his feet. His face was red with embarrassment. He made fists and glared at Elly May. "I'm gonna kill you!"

"No, I'm gonna kill *you!*" Elly May replied. She and Derek began to circle each other, but then the coach stepped in between them.

"No one kills anyone without a signed permission slip from home," he said.

Morgan grabbed Elly May by the arm and

started to pull her away. "Come on, practice is over anyway."

Elly May allowed herself to be pulled away, but her eyes never left Derek's. "I'll be back tomorrow," she said. "And then you'll be sorry."

FIFTEEN

The Clampetts may have become billionaires, but in many ways their lives had not changed. They were all still up at the crack of dawn doing chores long before the rest of Beverly Hills even heard their alarm clocks go off. Way out in the backyard, in her secret hiding place, Granny was putting the finishing touches on her still. As befitted a still in Beverly Hills, it was the largest and most ornate one she'd ever built.

"Just need to attach this shiny doohickey to that thingamabob so it points directly into the fancy widget," she said to herself as she screwed a brand-new gold-plated Kohler bathroom faucet onto a piece of copper pipe. "Then I'll get a little water from the cement pond, and Dr. Daisy May Moses will be open for business."

Back up at the mansion, the early-morning bustle had awakened Laura. Every morning she heard the bumpkins get up at the crack of dawn, but until now she'd never bothered to see what they did so early in the day. Today she decided to find out. Carrying a mug of steaming coffee, she stepped out the front door to find Jethro in the circular driveway working on his truck.

The tires were off it and the truck stood high in the air, supported at each corner by a Grecian statue. Jethro was attaching several round flashing lights to the chassis. Four huge black tires were piled on the ground nearby.

"Hey—" Laura quickly caught herself. "I mean, *bonjour*, Jethro. What is all this?"

"Oh, howdy, Miss Laurette," Jethro greeted her. "Miss Jane said a big, flashy car was more suitin' to my personality. I was watchin' TV yesterday and I saw the kind of truck she was talkin' about. So I figured I'd make my truck bigger and more flashy, just like the one I saw on TV."

He reached toward the dashboard and flicked a switch. Immediately the revolving lights began to flash. "So what do you think? Pretty flashy, huh?"

"I must say, it is wonderful!" Laura said. She couldn't believe what a moron he was! She walked around the side of the house and found Elly May standing on a ladder next to a giant satellite dish. She was holding a garden hose and splashing water into the meshlike dish.

"Elly May, what on earth are you doing?" Laura asked.

"I'm fillin' up this here birdbath," Elly May replied. "It's been empty ever since we moved in. Trouble is, as fast as I fill it up, it keeps drainin' out."

"Perhaps there is a leak," Laura said. She felt something alight on her shoulder. Looking around, she found that a pigeon had landed on her.

"Shoo, shoo!" She tried to chase the bird away, but he wouldn't leave.

"Looks like that little feller likes you," Elly May said.

There was nothing Laura could do about the damn bird, so she focused on Elly May instead. "He is adorable. But, Elly May, you must come down. It is time for your etiquette lesson."

"What are we studyin' up on today?" Elly May asked as she climbed down the ladder.

"Today I will teach you how to look interested when people are boring you," Laura said.

Suddenly she heard a small, plopping sound, and the pigeon took flight. Laura turned in horror and saw what the bird had left on her shoulder.

"Looks like he could use an etiquette lesson, too," Elly May said.

Later that morning Jethro went to work at the bank again. "Oh, Jethro." Hathaway waved from her office as he passed. "Come in here and see what I've done."

Jethro stepped into the office. Soft country music was coming from a small radio on a bookcase. Hathaway was sitting at her desk. Her hair was done up real pretty and she was wearing more makeup than she usually did. She pulled over an extra chair and patted it. "Come, Jethro, sit down."

Jethro sat and found himself staring at a computer screen.

"Now watch," Hathaway said as her fingers flew over a keyboard. Columns of words and numbers flashed onto the screen.

"As you can see, I've built on your visionary plan for finding your uncle a wife," she said. "First I created this rather modest database program. Then I cross-referenced the applicants against the parameters you indicated he desired by specifying the search criteria into functional groupings and selecting the field values through the use of embedded commands and, of course, basic Boolean algebra."

Jethro couldn't help grinning at her. "Miss Jane, I have to hand it to you. It looks like you done a great job."

"Oh, thank you, Jethro." Miss Hathaway gushed.

"There's just one small problem," Jethro said. "I have no idea what you're talking about."

"Oh, Jethro, you're so delightfully primitive," Miss Hathaway said affectionately. "All I meant was that I've narrowed the search for Uncle Jed's wife down to a few candidates."

"Well, hot dog, Miss Jane," Jethro said, filled with excitement. "I cain't wait to see them."

"I'd love to show them to you," Hathaway said. "But first let me run them by the chief. Whomever meets his approval I will introduce to your uncle Jed posthaste."

Hathaway's intercom lit up and buzzed.

"Excuse me for a moment, please," she said, and pressed the button. "Yes?"

"It's Drysdale, Hathaway. Come to my office right now, and bring the Arlington file with you."

"Right away, chief," Hathaway replied, getting up. Meanwhile Jethro bent over and scowled at the intercom.

"How'd Mr. Drysdale get in there?" he asked.

"You have a very funny sense of humor." Hathaway laughed. "I'm afraid I have to go." She grabbed the Arlington folder and headed for Drysdale's office.

Inside the office the bank president sat with Marilyn Arlington, a dazzling, beautiful woman in her midforties, with carefully coiffed black hair, expensive clothes, and ample amounts of jewelry. She had just handed Drysdale photographs of three beautiful thoroughbred horses.

"You know, Milburn," she said, "since I've trained three Kentucky Derby winners for other people, it seems logical that I should want to own and operate my own stud farm. I've decided to call it Arlington Acres."

"Stud farm." Drysdale nodded and handed the photos back. "Excellent idea."

Hathaway walked around the desk and handed Drysdale the folder. Then she stood at attention at his side, watching over his shoulder as he studied pictures of horses, financial print-outs, and various other documents.

"So, you agree that with Mr. Clampett's net worth and rural background, he would be the perfect partner for such a venture?" Ms. Arlington asked.

"Absolutely," Drysdale replied. "You and J. D. Clampett, partners in a stud farm."

"You'll call him and arrange for us to meet?" Ms. Arlington asked hopefully.

"You bet," Drysdale said. "I'll give him a ring as soon as you leave. I'm sure he'll want to see you right away."

Ms. Arlington rose and extended her hand. "I'm very excited about this."

"Me, too," Drysdale said, shaking her hand. "Thank you so much for coming in. I'll be in touch."

Hathaway and the bank's president watched the woman exit the office. As soon as she'd closed the door, Hathaway looked at her boss with a puzzled expression.

"I don't understand, chief," she said. "I thought you specifically told me you didn't want Mr. Clampett involved in any risky ventures."

"That's exactly right," Drysdale replied, handing the folder back to her. "Shred and burn this. And make sure that woman doesn't come anywhere near this office again."

"You're all heart, chief," Hathaway said with a smile.

Out near the reception desk, Jethro had just gone to get a new carton of pencils for his electronic whittling machine. As he crossed the reception area he noticed a striking woman on the phone.

"The meeting with Drysdale went fantastically!" she was saying. "He said I'd be the perfect partner for J. D. Clampett. Yes, yes, I'll tell you more when I get back."

Jethro looked her over. She sure was attractive. Just the kind of woman his uncle Jed was sure to like. And Jethro had no doubt that she'd be someone who'd be good at making Elly May more ladylike. She hung up the phone, and he decided to introduce himself.

"Excuse me, ma'am, but I'm Jethro Bodine, Mr. Clampett's nephew."

"Really?" The woman looked surprised, then delighted. "I'm Marilyn Arlington."

"Well, Miss Arlington, it sounds like Mr. Drysdale thinks you're the perfect match for my uncle Jed Clampett."

"That is what he said," Ms. Arlington said.

"Tell you what," Jethro said. "That bein' the case, why don't we mosey on over and meet my uncle right now?"

"Why, that sounds like a wonderful idea," Ms. Arlington said.

A little while later Jethro stood in the master bedroom with Jed and watched him straighten his tie. Jed had put on his courtin' suit.

"Ain't had much time to prepare for this," Jed said a little reluctantly.

"I know, Uncle Jed," Jethro said. "But that could be good. More spontaneouslike, you know?"

"I hope you're right," Jed said. "Anyway, I'm ready." He and Jethro started toward the door.

"I think you're gonna like Miss Arlington a lot," Jethro said as they stepped out onto the second-floor landing and started down the stairs. "Mr. Drysdale personally approved her himself."

"Well, now, I'm lookin' forward to gabbin' with her," Jed said, although the truth was that he was rather nervous about meeting a fancy Beverly Hills lady. They reached the foyer and stopped before a door that led to a sitting room. Jed paused and straightened his tie again. Then he pushed open the door.

Inside, Marilyn Arlington rose from a couch and extended her hand. Jed saw that she was both very beautiful and elegant. Never in his life would he have imagined marrying a woman like this. He felt his throat tighten a little and suddenly found it difficult to breathe.

"I'm delighted to meet you, Mr. Clampett," Ms. Arlington said, shaking his hand.

"Well, howdy, Miss Arlington," Jed said. "Gee, I don't know how to begin."

"Then let me start," Ms. Arlington said, stepping back and looking him over. "Mr. Clampett, I hope I'm not being too bold when I say this, but just by looking at you, I can tell that you're the perfect man for my stud farm."

Stud farm? Jed blinked. It was natural for a woman to want children, but a whole farm of them?

"Well, pardon me for sayin' this, ma'am, but that sounds like an overwhelmin' responsibility for an old country boy like myself."

"All right." Ms. Arlington took his response in stride. "If it will make it any easier for you, I'm willing to take on multiple partners."

Jed was shocked. He'd heard that Beverly Hills could be a pretty racy place, but he'd never expected anyone to be this forward about it. Heck, he and Miss Arlington weren't even married yet!

"Well, er, no offense, ma'am," he said. "But I think that might make me feel a tad uncomfortable."

"What if it was somebody you trusted?" Ms. Arlington asked. "Like Mr. Drysdale, for instance?"

"I couldn't imagine Mr. Drysdale wanting to get involved with something like that," Jed answered honestly.

Ms. Arlington just smiled. "Oh, I'm not so sure about that," she said. "You should have seen his face when I showed him pictures of what I have in mind. He was very excited."

Pictures!

"I don't doubt that," Jed mumbled.

"Maybe you'd like to see the pictures, too?" Ms. Arlington asked, reaching for her bag.

"Uh, not just yet," Jed replied quickly. "Don't you think we're going a little fast here?"

Ms. Arlington could see that Clampett was

the kind of man who needed to be nudged along. "Actually I don't think we're going fast enough. I've got the license and I'm ready to breed."

This was too much for Jed. "Excuse me, ma'am," he said. "I think I need some iced tea."

Eeeeeiiiinnnnm! They were suddenly interrupted by a high-pitched engine whine.

"Watch out, Jed!" Granny shouted from somewhere in the house.

Crash! Riding Jethro's dirt bike, Elly May crashed through the door of the sitting room.

"How do you stop this thang?" she shouted.

Before Jed could answer, she disappeared into the foyer. A second later Granny and Jethro raced into the sitting room and stopped to catch their breaths.

"I'm learnin' Elly May to ride my motor-sickle," Jethro shouted.

"When I catch that girl, I'm gonna tan her hide!" Granny shouted, waving her fist angrily.

Granny and Jethro raced out of the room. Suddenly Granny shouted, "Look out, Jed, she's comin' back!"

Jethro and Granny ran back into the sitting room and dived out of the way. A split second later Elly May raced through the room and back the way she'd come.

"You head her off that way, Granny," Jed shouted, pointing. "Jethro and me'll go this way."

Jed was just about to sprint out of the room when he noticed Ms. Arlington standing there with an astounded look on her face.

"Uh, Miss Arlington, if you could just hold your horses for one minute," he said.

"I got her!" Granny shouted from another room. "Look out! *Ooooooooo!*"

The dirt bike sped through the sitting room again, only this time Granny was riding it, and Elly May was chasing her. Jed and Jethro dashed after her.

"Hang on, Granny!" Jed shouted. "We're comin'!"

They chased Granny toward the indoor pool.

Ker-splash! There was a loud splash as the dirt bike and Granny sailed into the pool.

"I'll save ya!" Jethro shouted, and jumped into the pool after her. A moment later he emerged soaking wet with a dripping Granny kicking and cursing in his arms.

"Dagnammit! Dudgummed healot! Dadburn slap nabbit! Blue blazin' cruck flaggin' snuck mucker! Slinmg sloobin'! I'm het up, muled up, and fed up!"

Spanky, the orangutan, who'd been lounging by the pool, jumped out of his chair and ran away, covering his ears. Meanwhile Ms. Arlington had followed Jed and Elly May into the room by the pool. Looking sheepish, Elly May turned to her father.

"I'm sorry, Pa," she said.

"Elly May, look at your granny," Jed said sternly. "She's madder than a wet hen."

"Wetter, too," Jethro said, putting her down.

Jed turned back to his guest. "Miss Arlington, this here's my daughter, Elly May. You reckon, if we got hitched, you could help me tame her down some?"

"Are you proposing we get married?" Ms. Arlington asked, taken aback.

"Well, to be perfectly honest, ma'am, I wouldn't feel proper doin' all the breedin' you want to do if we wasn't," Jed said.

Ms. Arlington's jaw dropped. A second later she spun around in a huff and stormed out of the room.

"Now, what do you think got into her?" Jed wondered aloud.

SIXTEEN

That afternoon Elly May ran down the hall toward the Beverly Hills High School gym. She was late, and knew she'd probably missed most of wrestling practice. But she had a big date with Derek she was determined to keep. As she pushed through the doors and into the gym, the coach was just blowing his whistle.

"Okay, boys, that's the end of practice," he yelled. "Hit the mineral baths and don't forget to tip

the attendant. Also, I need a show of hands. How many of you have parents in the film industry?"

Almost every kid in the gym held up his hand.

"Great!" The coach started handing out eight-by-ten glossy photos of himself. "I just got my new head shots. Make sure you leave these where your parents can find them."

Elly May stood by the door and watched as the wrestlers headed for the locker room. Suddenly Derek spotted her.

"Well, well," he said. "Look who's here. It's the foxy boxer. Missed you at practice, babe."

"I couldn't make it," Elly May explained. "I had me an etiquette class today."

"Bawk, bawk, bawk." Derek made chicken sounds. "That's a new excuse for chickening out."

"I might have missed practice," Elly May said, "but I figured it would be okay to come down here afterward and wallop you anyway."

"Oh, yeah?" Derek turned toward her, looking very menacing. "We'll see about that."

As he and his buddies, Lance and Jake, stepped toward her, the gym door opened again and Morgan stepped through it.

"She didn't come alone," he said.

Derek and the others stared at Morgan in amused disbelief. "I'm sorry," Lance said. "But are we supposed to be scared?"

"Yeah," added Jake, "you can't be serious, *Organ*."

"I'll take the babe," Derek grumbled. "You guys get the Organ."

"He didn't come alone either," Elly May said. Behind her the gym door opened again and through it came about twenty kids.

Derek suddenly stopped and stared. All those kids had one thing in common. They were all kids he'd picked on.

"We just wanted to keep things fair," Elly May said.

Lance and Jake began to step back.

"Uh, you're on your own, Derek," Lance muttered.

Derek puffed out his chest and tried to look brave. "So what are you planning to do?"

Elly May peeled off her clothes. Underneath she was wearing a one-piece wrestling uniform.

"I plan to rassle," she spit out.

Derek smiled. "Well, then come on."

They headed toward the main wrestling mat. Meanwhile Morgan and the others climbed into the bleachers. Within moments word of the fight had spread throughout the school and the surrounding neighborhood via cellular phones, faxes, and computers. There was a fight in the gym and it couldn't be missed.

Kids were still streaming into the stands as Elly May and Derek went into a clinch.

Whomp! Elly May picked him up and threw

him down hard against the mat. Before Derek knew what was happening, she'd twisted him into an incredibly contorted and painful hold.

"This here's what I call the Clampett Clamp!" Elly May growled.

"It's not legal!" Derek croaked. "Illegal move!"

"Oh, yeah?" said Elly May. "Then try this one. I call it the Possum Pretzel."

She twisted him into a different position.

"That's not legal, either," Derek gasped.

"Okay, then how about the Hickory-Nut Crunch?" Elly May asked, twisting him in yet another direction. The kids in the stands shouted encouragement.

"That's definitely not legal!" Derek said, his voice becoming high-pitched.

"Ain't nothin' legal around here?" Elly May asked.

"Let me up and I'll show you," Derek said.

"Okay." Elly May jumped up and stood with her hands on her hips. Derek struggled to his feet and lunged at her. Elly May let him take her down and pin her shoulders to the mat.

"Elly May!" Morgan cried from the bleachers. "What are you doing?"

Above her Derek grinned triumphantly and counted. "One, two . . ."

Suddenly Elly May squirmed out of his grip and flipped him over, reversing the hold. Derek stared up at her in shock.

"Now, don't tell me this one ain't legal," Elly May said. "Because it's the same darn hold you just used on me. Now let's see. That's one . . . two . . . Now, what do you do after you say two?"

"Say three!" Morgan yelled from the bleachers.

"Three!" Elly May shouted.

The crowd of spectators started to cheer. Still pinned, Derek twisted around and shouted at Jake and Lance. "Help me, you guys!"

Derek's friends started toward the mat, but before they got there, Elly May picked up Derek and threw him into them.

Thud! Crunch! Derek slammed into his friends and they all fell to the floor in a heap. Elly May stood over them.

"You're just lucky Granny wasn't here," she said. "She fights dirty."

The coach stormed out of the locker room, looking furious.

"Young lady!" he shouted angrily.

"Yes?" Elly May trembled, but the coach suddenly smiled.

"I just wanted to tell you that I think we've found ourselves a new team captain," he said. He turned to Derek. "Sorry, Derek, you've been demoted."

Jake and Lance struggled to their feet and helped pull up a dejected-looking Derek.

"Man," he muttered in defeat. "Imagine being replaced by a girl."

* * *

Meanwhile the crowd lifted Elly May to their shoulders and cheered even louder. Morgan wanted to join them, but the coach grabbed him by the arm.

"Did you see how I did it?" the coach asked.

"Did what?" Morgan said with a frown.

"Well, first I made believe I was angry at Elly May," the coach said. "Then I did a dramatic turn, and was happy. I think it made the moment more powerful, don't you?"

"Oh, yeah, sure," Morgan said.

"Here's one of my new head shots," the coach said. "Your father's in the movie business, isn't he?"

"No, he's a bank president," Morgan said.

"Oh." The coach looked disappointed. Then he brightened. "Well, he must have movie-star clients!"

"I bet he does," Morgan said with a nod. "But based on what I just saw, I have a piece of advice for you."

"What's that?" the coach asked.

"Don't quit your day job."

SEVENTEEN

That night the Beverly Wilshire Hotel was brightly lit in anticipation of a celebration that would rival the Academy Awards. Searchlights arced back and forth across the sky and valet parkers scurried around, parking long black limousines.

Inside the grand ballroom, huge crystal chandeliers shimmered. Waiters carried silver trays of hors d'oeuvres and fluted glasses filled with sparkling champagne. A huge banner hung high above the room:

HAPPY 50TH BIRTHDAY, JED CLAMPETT

Dressed in a brand-new gown bought specifically for the occasion, Margaret Drysdale stared up at the banner and then at her husband beside her. "I still don't understand it, Milburn," she said.

"Don't understand what?" Milburn Drysdale asked.

"Why we have to throw this outrageously expensive party for that hillbilly," Margaret said.

"Well, Margaret," Drysdale replied. "I can give you about a billion reasons why."

"And where did you find all these people?"

"Most of them are out-of-work movie extras," Drysdale said.

Outside the hotel Hathaway drove up and got out of her Miata. She stepped uncertainly on heels that were somewhat higher than those on the sensible shoes she normally wore.

Beep! Beep! The loud blare of a car horn startled her and she jumped around.

"Oh, my goodness!" she gasped in awe. Behind her was Jethro's truck, only now it had huge wheels and rode nearly ten feet off the ground. Riding atop it was Jethro, Jed, and Granny in their best Sunday clothes.

"Howdy, Miss Jane." Jethro waved down at her. "I took your advice and made me a big fancy car. It's just like them ones on TV."

"It suits you, Jethro." Hathaway clutched her hands together. "It's very macho."

Jethro let out a rope ladder, and they helped Granny climb down. Jed followed, and Jethro came last, carrying a covered dish, which he handed back to Granny when he got to the ground.

"Made something special for the party," Granny told Hathaway. "Possum shanks."

"That's very sweet of you, Granny," Hathaway said. The four of them entered the crowded ballroom, and Jethro spotted the long row of buffet tables along the far wall.

"Yee-ha!" he cried happily. "Vittles!"

He took off across the room like a pro fullback running through a team of second-graders. People literally dived out of his way. As he passed the Drysdales Margaret looked at her husband in shock.

"Ah," Milburn Drysdale said with a sigh. "It appears that the Clampetts have arrived."

As Jethro neared the buffet tables he saw Miss Laurette all done up pretty and talking to a fancy blond lady in a black evening gown. The woman's back was toward Jethro, but he had no doubt that she was a movie star. No doubt, that was, until she turned around.

It was Elly May!

"Weee-doggies!" Jethro said with a grin. His cousin was all dolled up with makeup and jewelry and high heels, and looked beautiful. Now Jed and Granny caught up to them.

"Why, howdy," Elly May started to say. Then she caught herself. "I mean, good evening, Pa. Good evening, Granny."

She kissed Granny the French way, giving her a little peck on either side of her face. Jed couldn't get over the transformation in his daughter's appearance.

"You look plumb elegant, Elly May," he said proudly.

"Thanks, Pa," Elly May replied, slightly embarrassed. "I feel funny gettin' all gussied up like this. But Miss Laurette says I'll get used to it."

"I reckon you're doin' a fine job turnin' Elly May into a lady," Jed told Laura.

"*Merci,* Monsieur Clampett," Laura replied.

"Well, all I knows is she ain't gonna be able to run in them shoes," Granny said.

Margaret and Milburn Drysdale approached them.

"Well, howdy, Mr. and Mrs. Drysdale," Jed said, offering his hand. "Thanks for throwing this here shindig for me."

"It's our pleasure," Drysdale said, turning to his wife. "Right, Margaret?"

"Absolutely," his wife replied. "We're both thrilled and delighted."

Granny held up her covered dish for Margaret to see. "I just wanted you to know we didn't come empty-handed. I cooked up a mess of possum shanks. I'll put 'em with the rest of the fixin's. And don't you worry if we run out, Miz Drysdale. I made an extra batch just for you."

Margaret Drysdale glanced through the glass top of the dish and turned a green-tinted shade of white. Meanwhile Jethro was working his way down the buffet table, throwing samples of each offering on his plate. Suddenly he stopped and scowled.

"May I help you?" asked a waiter standing behind the table.

"Yeah," Jethro said, pointing down at three serving platters. "What all's this stuff?"

"Why, this is sushi," the waiter said. "That's calamari, and that's caviar."

"Pardon me," Jethro said, "but could you say that in American?"

"Why, of course," the waiter said with a smile. "This is raw fish. That's baby squid, and that's salted fish eggs."

"You sure this stuff belongs here?" Jethro asked.

"Why, of course, sir," said the waiter. "Why do you ask?"

"Well, this seems like a pretty fancy shindig for puttin' out fish bait," Jethro said. "On the other hand, when you're as hungry as I am, you'll eat just about anything."

He proceeded to pile large helpings on his plate and moved down to the next offering, where he bumped into Hathaway.

"Why, howdy again, Miss Jane," he said with a grin as he stuffed some crepes into his pocket.

"Hello, Jethro," Hathaway said. "Taking something home for Duke?"

Jethro patted his pockets. "Heck, no, Miss Jane. This is all for me. Duke don't eat fish bait."

Hathaway nodded, exhibiting a level of toleration only those in love can feel. "So, I've been meaning to ask you something, Jethro. Perhaps after your uncle finds a wife, it will be your turn to look for a mate."

"Me?" Jethro looked surprised. "Get married? No, ma'am, I wanna be one of them Hollywood bachelors and date all the starlets."

Hathaway was disappointed, but somehow not surprised. "Well, let me remind you not to overlook the charms of the slightly older woman, who more than makes up with experience what she may lack in other areas."

Jethro gave her a blank look, not at all certain of what she'd just said. Then he nodded. "If you say so, Miss Jane."

Having left Elly May with her father and

Granny, Laura walked along one of the walls. The branches of a potted plant suddenly parted, and Tyler stuck his face out.

"Hey, Laura!" he whispered with a smirk.

Laura froze and stepped up close to the plant. "What are *you* doing here?"

"I wanted to see what was going on," Tyler whispered. "We're partners in this, remember, Laura?"

"Oh, right, of course. How could I forget?" Laura said. "And for God's sake, don't call me Laura. I'm Miss Laurette, the French tutor."

Two attractive women walked by, talking about Jed.

"I hear he's quite eager to get married," said one.

"I wonder what he's looking for in a wife?" the other asked. They both sounded very interested.

Tyler stuck his head through the plant again, surprising the women. "I hear he's interested in how many peas a person can stick up their nose," he said. "It must be a hillbilly thing."

The women looked shocked. "Well, he can forget about me," one huffed.

"Me, too," said the other.

"That was rather clever, Tyler," Laura said.

"I've been bad-mouthing Clampett everywhere," Tyler said. "But believe me, there are plenty of women around who'll put up with a lot for a billion dollars."

"Don't worry so much," Laura said. "The way I got Elly May to look tonight, Jed Clampett must think I'm the greatest thing since *Hee-haw*."

"Now, *that* was a good show," Tyler said.

"Shh." Laura pressed her finger to her lips. She'd just caught sight of Elly May coming across the room toward her.

"Get lost, Tyler," Laura whispered. "It's time for me to play my ace in the hole."

Tyler let the branches close. Laura looked sad and dabbed her eyes with a cocktail napkin. As she came closer Elly May looked concerned. "Are you okay, Miss Laurette?"

"*Oui,* Elly May," Laura said with a sniff.

"Well, if you say you're okay, how come you're crying?" Elly May asked.

"It is not important," Laura replied.

"Sure, it is."

"No, really, I want you to enjoy yourself tonight," Laura said. "Do not worry about me."

"Well, I cain't enjoy myself when you look so unhappy," Elly May said. "So why don't you just tell me what's wrong?"

Laura took a deep breath and let it out slowly. "All right. It is just that I have spoken to your father. And he says that I for him would make the best wife."

"You and Pa?" Elly May's jaw dropped.

"I knew you wouldn't like it." Laura shook her head sadly.

"That's not true!" Elly May said. "I was just surprised, that's all."

"Well, as happy as I would make your father," Laura said, "I told him I did not wish to displease you. Perhaps you should talk to him."

"Why, I'll do that," Elly May said with a nod. A waiter carrying a tray of champagne passed, and Elly May took a glass and handed it to Laura.

"Here you are, Miss Laurette," she said. "This will help calm your nerves."

"Why, *merci,* Elly May," Laura said.

"Now I'm gonna go find my pa and have a word with him," Elly May said.

"Wait!" Laura momentarily forgot her French accent. "Oh, er, I mean, don't talk to him right now. Wait a little while." She gave Elly May a wink.

"If you say so." Elly May winked back. "I was thinkin' of goin' outside and restin' my feet anyway. These here high heels sure do cause some achin' for a girl's feet. See you later."

Elly May went off. Laura looked down at the champagne glass in her hand. She was tempted to drink some, but then thought better of it. This was an important evening, and she had to keep her edge. She quickly dumped the champagne in the plant, dousing Tyler in the face.

Tyler licked his lips. "Hmmm. Cheap champagne. Drysdale must've bought it."

Laura waited a few moments and then

walked across the ballroom floor, where she joined Jed. Together they watched Elly May go through a door and disappear.

"Elly May looks lovely tonight, don't you agree, Monsieur Clampett?" Laura said.

"I sure do," Jed said. "And I truly thank you for all you've taught her."

"She is a wonderful girl," Laura said wistfully. "I will miss her so much when you find yourself a wife. And, you know, I will miss you, too."

Jed's eyebrows went up. "I hadn't thought of you not being around, Miss Laurette. It's been such a pleasure having you stay with us."

"You are too kind, Monsieur Clampett," Laura said. "You know, Elly May said the funniest thing tonight. She said she would be very disappointed if you chose someone other than me to be her mother. But I am sure she was only teasing."

"It's not like Elly May to tease," Jed said, rubbing his chin thoughtfully. "And I'd sure hate to think of disappointin' the girl."

"Perhaps you should have a talk with her," Laura suggested.

"I reckon I'll do that," Jed said. "Thanks, Miss Laurette. I'll go talk to her right now."

He turned and went off through the same door Elly May had gone through a few moments before. He found her out on a balcony, sitting on a bench, barefoot. Her high heels sat on the ground next to her, and she was feeding two squirrels.

"I hope I ain't disturbin' you," Jed said, touching her shoulder tenderly.

"You ain't, Pa," Elly May replied sweetly. "I just had to take my shoes off and rest my feet for a spell."

"That's okay, Elly May," Jed said, sitting down beside her. "This here's a big night for you. You're all growed up and ladylike at your first Beverly Hills shindig. I'm tellin' you, girl, your ma would sure be proud."

"Thanks, Pa." Elly May squeezed his hand affectionately. "Miss Laurette said she was right proud, too."

"You like her, don't you?" Jed asked.

"I like her just fine, Pa. And I guess you like her, too."

"I certainly do," Jed said. "I just want you to be happy, Elly May."

"I just want you to be happy, too," Elly May said.

"Well, then that about settles it," Jed said. If it would make Elly May happy to see Miss Laurette become her mother, then Jed would be glad to do it.

The door opened, and Jethro stuck his head out. "Hey, Uncle Jed, you gotta come in. They're bringin' out a big ol' birthday cake for you."

Elly May quickly slipped her high heels back

on and hopped up. "Come on, Pa, you cain't miss this." She grabbed her father's hand and pulled him off the bench.

A few moments later Jed stood in the center of the ballroom and watched as a huge cake was pushed toward him. An artist had used different-colored icings to draw his picture on the cake, and the whole thing was encircled by fifty candles. The crowd around Jed began to sing "Happy Birthday" and then clapped loudly as he took a big breath and blew all the candles out.

"Whew!" He gasped for breath. "It sure takes a bit more breath to blow these candles out than it used to."

People chuckled and then quieted as if waiting for a speech. Jed realized the spotlight was on him.

"Well . . ." He paused and cleared his throat nervously. "I want to thank Mr. and Mrs. Drysdale for going through all this trouble just for me. A man couldn't ask for finer neighbors. And even though I don't know most of y'all, I'm glad you're here. I have more than any man deserves, and yet there's one thing more I'd like to ask for on my birthday."

"A yacht?" someone in the crowd muttered, but the others quickly shushed him. Jed turned to Hathaway.

"Now, Miss Hathaway, I'm sure you would've introduced me to many fine Beverly Hills ladies if

I gave you the chance, but I think I've made up my mind about who I'm gonna ask to marry me. I'd like to ask the one who helped my daughter, Elly May, become a lady—Miss Laurette."

"Me?" Laura cried dramatically. "But I am so surprised."

"That is, if you'll have me," Jed said with a shy grin.

Laura ran through the crowd and threw her arms around Jed's neck. As they kissed, the crowd burst into applause. In the back of the room, Woodrow Tyler did a little victory dance.

The only person who didn't appear pleased was Granny, who took a nip from her flask and muttered, "I just don't trust her. I don't, I don't, I don't."

EIGHTEEN

Hathaway's forehead was furrowed with wrinkles of worry the next morning as she waited outside Drysdale's office.

"Come in, Hathaway," the bank president called. He was feeling quite chipper. "It's a great day for the bank—no thanks to you. Hors d'oeuvres?"

He pressed a paper plate toward her. On it were a dozen wilted hors d'oeuvres from the night before.

"No, thank you." Hathaway settled down in a chair and thumbed nervously through some papers. "Chief, I'm sure you agree that we should be proceeding with caution on this new development regarding Mr. Clampett."

"Oh, don't be so skeptical, Hathaway," Drysdale said irritably. "Did anyone ever tell you that you have a real tendency to depress people?"

Hathaway chose to ignore the question. "But I haven't even done a computer analysis on this woman," she said. "What do we know about her?"

"We know that she's going to make J. D. Clampett happy," Drysdale replied. "And a happy billionaire keeps his money in my bank. Stop thinking of yourself, Hathaway. Start thinking of me."

"But, chief, I feel a certain responsibility," Hathaway protested. "As you know, my marital endeavors—"

"—haven't amounted to a hill of beans." Drysdale finished the sentence for her. "But don't worry. Clampett's decided to give you a second chance. He wants you to be in charge of planning his wedding for him."

"What's to plan?" Hathaway asked. "I overheard Laurette saying she either wanted to elope or have a small, private affair as soon as possible."

"Impossible!" Drysdale slapped the desktop with his hand. "This man is the richest person in Beverly Hills. Everyone knows he's my client. If it's not a big, fancy wedding, *I'm* the one who looks bad. You're to take care of everything, from contacting the media to arranging security."

"But they want the wedding immediately," Hathaway said.

"Then you'll do it immediately," Drysdale commanded.

"But, I mean, in two days," Hathaway tried to explain.

"Then you'll do it in two days!" Drysdale shouted.

Hathaway nodded. It was going to be an enormous job.

Drysdale bit into one of the day-old hors d'oeuvres and grimaced. "And one other thing, Hathaway. Get better hors d'oeuvres this time. It's his money we're spending, not mine."

Back at the Clampett mansion, Jed was collecting eggs from the gazebo he and Elly May had converted into a chicken coop. Woodrow Tyler, wearing a suit and tie and holding a large manila envelope, approached.

"Uh, excuse me, Mr. Clampett," he said.

Jed looked up and scowled. "You ain't another insurance salesman, are you?"

"No, sir, I'm from the bank," Tyler said, taking a white, typewritten document from the envelope. "Remember? I brought Granny the flowers."

"Oh, yes." Jed nodded. "Well, what can I do for you, son?"

Tyler handed him the papers. "Miss Hathaway sent me with this document for you to sign."

"Oh, yeah? What's it say?" Jed asked.

"It's just a standard prenuptial agreement," Tyler said, holding out a pen. "Miss Hathaway said that you shouldn't tell anyone you've signed it. Not even her."

"Well, if it's from Miss Hathaway, I'm sure it's just fine," Jed said, putting the eggs down.

Tyler bent over, and Jed laid the document on his back and signed it. Trying not to seem too eager, Tyler took the document back and gestured at the chicken-coop gazebo.

"These are some lucky chickens to have such a fine coop, sir," he said hastily. "Well, I've got to scoot."

He ran back to his car and took off down the driveway. Jed watched and shook his head. "Boy, these young fellers are always actin' like they's two steps ahead of a stampede."

Around the back of the mansion, Granny spoke to Pearl on one of them newfangled cellular phones. She'd just lit a fire under her still, which now stood about fifteen feet in the air and sparkled in the California sun.

A thousand miles from Beverly Hills, back in the misty hills of the Ozarks, Pearl sat in a chair, her face covered with a cold-cream mask. She was talking on an old, black rotary-dial phone while Jethrine, just back from beautician's school, put curlers in her mother's hair. As Jethro's twin, Jethrine was the spitting image of her brother— just as tall, just as strong, and just as dumb.

"Hold on, Granny, I want to tell Jethrine," Pearl said, turning to her daughter. "Guess what? Your uncle Jed's gettin' married."

"Oh, I always cry at weddings." Jethrine sniffed just at the thought of it. Pearl got back on the phone.

"Who's he marrying?" she asked.

"Some floozy with a fancy accent," Granny said. "She seems sneaky, and I don't trust her."

"You don't trust anybody," Pearl reminded her.

"Well, never mind that," Granny said. "I'm invitin' y'all and the cousins. But just from Jed's side. Not including the Kellogs nor the Stonewalls nor the Daggetts. Not that the Daggetts is so bad, but they're twice removed from Jed."

"Now, you're not gonna take to your medicine and disappear like ya did when Jed married your daughter, are you?" Pearl asked.

"Maybe I will, and maybe I won't," Granny replied. "Now I gotta go, Pearl. Looks like my new medicine is startin' to flow."

Granny hung up and turned back to her still. The fire burned beneath it, and from the end of the gold bathroom faucet, clear liquid began to drip into a fancy china teacup. Granny smiled to herself.

"They'll be comin' from miles around to get my expert doctorin'," she said to herself. "I won't turn a one away. I done took me the hypocritter oath to help everyone."

Granny picked up the teacup and poured a few drops on a withered rosebush in the garden. As soon as the clear liquid touched it, the bush instantly blossomed and bloomed.

"Hmmm." Granny sniffed the teacup. "Kinda weak, but probably good enough for city folk."

Suddenly she heard a rustling in the bushes nearby. Looking up, she spotted Miss Laurette wearing a long red scarf, sneaking through the shrubs. Sensing she was up to no good, Granny started to follow her. Pretty soon Miss Laurette stopped by a wall. A moment later some feller wearing a dark suit scrambled over it. Granny recognized him as the feller from the bank who'd brought her those flowers.

Unaware that they were being watched, Laura and Tyler huddled near the wall.

"Did he sign it?" Laura asked eagerly.

"Oh, yeah," Tyler said. "Jed Clampett's a very trusting man. He actually thinks everyone's honest."

"Good," Laura said. "That's a quality I admire in the person I'm taking advantage of."

"Just tell me one thing," Tyler said. "Tell me you're not sleeping with him."

"Come on, Woodrow," Laura replied. "You know that once I move in with someone, I stop having sex with them."

"Oh, yeah, that's right." Woodrow had forgotten.

"Now go," Laura said.

"Hey, I did good work," Tyler said. "How about one little kiss as a reward?"

"Okay, but only to tease you," Laura said. She puckered her lips and planted a short one on Tyler's lips.

Suddenly the bushes shook and Granny jumped up, pointing a finger at them.

"I knew it!" she yelled triumphantly. "I just knew it! I caught you red-handed, you two-timin' hussy. You ain't even French! Wait till I tell Jed! You can forget about that wedding, Miss Laurette!"

"Get her!" Laura ordered.

"Uh-oh!" Granny turned and started to run, but Tyler raced up behind and tackled her. Granny kicked and scratched, but Tyler held her on the ground and wrapped his tie around her mouth so she couldn't yell. Laura used her scarf to tie Granny's hands behind her back.

"Well, Mama Yokum," Laura said in a mocking country twang, "looks like there ain't gonna be no possum stew tonight!"

Granny squirmed and twisted, but it was no use. She couldn't get free.

"What do we do with her?" Tyler asked.

"The car," Laura said.

They picked up Granny and threw her over the wall, and then climbed over it themselves. A few moments later they threw her in the backseat of Tyler's car. Laura and Tyler got in the front. Tyler drove.

"So, tell me, Tyler," Laura said. "Now that we got Gomer to sign the papers, how long is it going to take to transfer his money to the Swiss bank account?"

"I've already input the transaction information into my computer," Tyler replied. "As soon as you say 'I do,' I press enter and bing! The signal goes through the modem to Switzerland, and we're rich!"

"And Clampett's on the next train back to Bumpkinville," Laura said with a smirk. She stretched out in the car, and Tyler glanced down at her incredibly long, beautiful legs.

"Oh, man, look at those gams," he moaned. "I can't wait to have them wrapped around me."

Suddenly Granny's legs flew over the backseat and scissored around Tyler's neck, choking him.

"Get her off me!" Tyler cried, trying to pry the old lady's legs off with one hand while driving with the other.

Laura reached around and managed to pull Granny's legs off Tyler.

"Jeez, what are we gonna do with her?" Tyler asked, rubbing his sore neck. Just at that moment they passed a large gray building with a cement ramp leading up to the front door. A sign out front said LOS VIEJOS RETIREMENT HOME

"I just got an idea," Laura said.

A little while later Laura, Tyler, and Granny sat in the office of Myron Mackey, the retirement home's director. Mackey was a short, balding man with an unemotional expression and a face that looked like a basset hound's. Granny was still writhing and squirming, but Tyler had reinforced the bonds that held her. Laura dabbed her eyes with a handkerchief, and Tyler looked very grim.

"She doesn't even think we're her grand-children anymore," Laura said with a sniff.

Mackey nodded as he jotted down some notes. "And you say you fear for your lives?"

"Yes," said Tyler. "I'm afraid the poor old dear tried to shoot us with a shotgun. Lucky for us, she's a terrible shot."

"Mmmmmmppphhhhh!" Granny struggled and shook her head furiously.

"Are there any other indications of dementia?" Mackey asked.

"Yes," said Laura. "She's convinced that she lives in a mansion in Beverly Hills."

"I see." Mackey jotted down more notes.

"And last week we even caught her eating a raccoon," Tyler added.

"Really." Mackey took the news gravely.

"She calls us kidnappers," Laura sobbed.

"They *are* kidnappers!" Granny suddenly shouted. She'd managed to work the tie off her mouth, but Tyler quickly jumped up and tightened it again. In the process Granny bit him on the hand.

"Ow!" Tyler shouted.

Mackey quickly pressed a button on his intercom. "I need two orderlies, stat!"

"She bit me again!" Tyler moaned, holding his throbbing hand. "You may want to test her for rabies, Mr. Mackey. I know it's a problem among raccoons."

Two young men in white uniforms rushed into the office.

"Sedate her," Mackey said, pointing at Granny. The young men picked her up and carried her off kicking and writhing.

"We can't stand to have our hearts broken again," Laura said, dabbing her eyes. "We need to place her somewhere that will keep her in a straitjacket, and away from sharp objects and pay phones."

"I agree," Mackey said. "From what you've

told me, I'd say your grandmother is a perfect candidate for electroshock therapy."

Laura smiled behind her handkerchief. "I knew we came to the right place."

The following day various members of the Clampett clan gathered in the living room of the mansion, along with Hathaway and half a dozen nervous-looking professional wedding organizers. Elly May had dressed up Spanky, the orangutan, in a tuxedo.

"Now, Spanky," she said, "if I have to get all spiffed up tomorrow and be the bridesmaid, then you have to get spiffed up, too. Especially you being the ring bearer and all."

The orangutan put his arm around Elly May and kissed her forehead.

"Aw, you're such a sweet talker," Elly May said with a sigh.

Across the room Hathaway paced back and forth before the wedding organizers, who were all scribbling frantically on notepads and typing madly on laptop computers. Jed sat off to the side, listening to everything while he calmly whittled.

"Most important," Hathaway said in a commanding voice. "Nobody, I repeat, *nobody* is to be allowed into the Clampett estate tomorrow without an invitation. Also, I just inspected the din-

ing tent, and I want it moved two feet to the north. And the spittoons go on the groom's side."

The door from the kitchen swung open, and an upset-looking man wearing a white apron hurried out shouting in French. Jethro followed him.

"What's the problem?" Hathaway asked.

"This here feller's all upset because I threw out a box of weddin' food," Jethro explained. "The box was marked es-car-got, but when I opened it, there weren't nothin' in there but a bunch of snails. They must've ate up all the food."

"It's no problem, Jethro. We'll just order some more." Hathaway snapped her fingers at the French chef. *"Henri, vite! Allez!"*

The cellular phone in her briefcase rang, and Hathaway answered it. "Uh-huh . . . uh-huh . . . Wait, I'll ask him." She put her hand over the phone and turned to Jed. "It's the dressmaker. Granny didn't show up for her fitting. If she doesn't hurry, she'll never have her dress in time for the wedding tomorrow."

"I ain't seen hide nor hair of Granny since yesterday," Jed said.

"Aren't you worried?" Hathaway asked.

"About Granny?" Jed smiled and shrugged. "Heck, no. She did the same thing when I married Elly May's ma. Went off on a bender and dragged

herself in three days later naked as a jaybird and reekin' of her medicine."

Hathaway raised a skeptical eyebrow. It seemed odd to her that Granny would miss this wedding.

NINETEEN

The day of the wedding had finally arrived. At dawn, out at the airport, a jet from Little Rock landed with ninety-seven hillbillies aboard. As they filed off, carrying banjos, jugs of moonshine and gift-wrapped goats, Jethrine Bodine paused beside a stewardess.

"Excuse me, ma'am," she said, "but I've always wanted to fly into the clouds and visit faraway places. How do I get to be a flight attendant?"

The stewardess stared up at Jethro's twin sister, horrified by the notion. "Well, it's very competitive. And there are height and weight restrictions."

"But beautiful gals like us always get first crack," Jethrine said with a wink.

The stewardess nodded in wide-eyed disbelief. That hillbilly was one of the largest and most unattractive women she'd ever seen. Next, Hank and Frank passed by wearing their skunk-skin hats, and then came Mayor Jasper and Spittin' Sam.

"Hey, Spittin' Sam," Jasper said. "Y'all hear whether or not Cousin Bill's comin' to the weddin'?"

"I heard he wanted to," Spittin' Sam replied. "But darn old Hillary said he cain't come."

"Darn," said Jasper. "Someone's got to tell that girl who wears the pants in that family."

"You can tell her," Spittin' Sam replied. "I sure ain't."

Back at the Clampett estate, Hathaway stepped out into the early-morning sun to survey the property one last time and make sure everything was in order. As she walked toward the back of the grounds, she spotted something hidden in the shrubs . . . something she'd never noticed before. At first she thought it was some sort of freestanding sculpture. But as she got closer she realized it was a still. Then a glint of metal caught her eye. Lying nearby in the grass was Granny's flask.

Hathaway picked it up, remembering how Granny had said she never left home without it. Hathaway knew at once that she should have trusted her instincts. Granny hadn't gone off on a bender. Something was wrong!

There wasn't much time before the wedding. Hathaway raced into town and paid a quick trip to the Beverly Hills police, where she met with Captain Gallo, the man who'd led the siege on the Clampett mansion when Jed and his family had first arrived.

"Sorry, Miss Hathaway," Gallo said with a shrug. "If the immediate family isn't concerned enough to file a missing-persons' report, then there's not much we can do."

Hathaway carefully weighed her options. She knew she could get Jed or Elly May to file the report, but she didn't want to upset them on such an important day.

"If you can't help me, is there anyone who can?" she asked.

"Well, if you're *that* desperate . . ." Gallo slid open the drawer of his desk and took out a card. "He's expensive, but he's also the best private investigator around."

There wasn't much time. The detective's name was Jones. Hathaway phoned him with

the information, then went back to the mansion.

A few hours later she stepped into Mr. Jones's office. She froze as he turned to face her.

"Something wrong?" the gray-haired private detective asked.

"I feel like I've seen you before somewhere," Hathaway said.

Jones nodded. "Lot of people say that. There must be some TV detective from the seventies I remind people of."

"I bet that's it," Hathaway said.

"Anyway, have a seat, Miss Hathaway," Jones said, gesturing to a chair.

Hathaway sat down. "Have you discovered anything?" she asked impatiently. The wedding was only hours away.

"Oh, this case was pretty easy to crack, Miss Hathaway," Jones said. "I've met some unsavory characters before, but this one takes the cake."

"What do you mean?" Hathaway asked anxiously.

Jones tossed an eight-by-ten-glossy black-and-white photo across the desk. "Laurette Voleur, also known as Laura Jackson, also know as Lilly LaBeck. Married twelve times, each time to a guy with some extra money to throw around."

"I should have known!" Hathaway said.

"She usually finds some patsy to help her," Jones said. "If you want to know who it is, I'll need a little more time."

"But what about Granny?" Hathaway asked.

"The old lady is being held against her will at the Los Viejos Retirement Home. It's a pretty disreputable place often cited for patient abuse. It'll be tough to break her out."

"What a calamity!" Hathaway cried. "The wedding's only hours away!"

She jumped up and took out her checkbook. "Whom should I make your fee out to?" she asked.

"Jones," the detective said. "Barnaby Jones."

Moments later, outside the private detective's office, Hathaway pulled out her trusty cellular phone. There wasn't a moment to lose.

Meanwhile, over at the Clampett mansion, everyone was bustling around, attending to last-minute wedding details. In the midst of it all, Laura, in her wedding gown, slipped out into a second-floor hallway and met with Tyler, who'd snuck in unnoticed.

"All right, we're starting soon," she whispered. "Get the modem hooked up. As soon as that preacher says 'I now pronounce you man and wife,' you push that button. The cash gets wired to Switzerland, and I say good-bye to Hillbilly Hell."

"Good, good," Tyler said. "Maybe I should check to make sure your garter belt is on straight."

"Get out of here," Laura snapped, slapping his hands away. "And don't let anyone see you."

Tyler turned and started down the stairs. The place was filled with caterers, maids, and delivery boys. Tyler knew that if he just acted natural, he probably wouldn't get caught. As he reached the foyer a phone near him started to ring. Tyler froze in his tracks as a maid answered.

"Hello, Clampett residence," she said. "Okay, wait, I'll see." She put her hand over the phone and called out, "Is there a Mr. Drysdale here? I have an urgent call from a Miss Hathaway."

Hathaway? Tyler had a funny feeling about that. "I'll take that," he said. "I work with Mr. Drysdale."

The maid handed him the phone. "Hello, Hathaway, it's Tyler."

"Tyler?" Hathaway was puzzled. "What are you doing at the Clampetts'?"

"I just dropped by a little early to see if I could be of help," Tyler said.

"Well, this is an extreme emergency," Hathaway said over her cellular phone. "Is Mr. Drysdale there?"

"I'm afraid not, but I'd be happy to take a message."

"Oh, all right, I guess you'll have to," Hathaway said. "But this is extremely important, Tyler. You must tell the chief to stop the wedding. Laurette Voleur is a con artist who's only after Mr. Clampett's money. It's going to take me a little while, but I'll be there as soon as I can. So tell the chief what I just told you, or your job is history."

"Hey, you can count on me," Tyler said, and hung up.

Outside, two large yellow-and-white-striped tents had been set up. One was the wedding tent for the ceremony. The other was the party tent, set up beside the outdoor pool for the party that would follow the ceremony. Both were filled with magnificent flowers and decorations.

Under the party tent, Milburn Drysdale and his family were inspecting the decorations. While Milburn stopped to sample some of the hors d'oeuvres, Margaret fed one to Babette. The dog wolfed it down and barked for another. Morgan, holding the poodle's leash, had to restrain the dog.

"Milburn," Margaret said, "Babette's been acting very strangely."

"That's because you're feeding her too much," Drysdale snapped. "Look at how fat she is."

"Dad's right, Mom," Morgan said. "Babette's turning into a real porker."

"Where is Hathaway?" Drysdale asked, staring at his watch. "She was supposed to check in with me hours ago."

"Maybe Babette ate her," Morgan muttered.

Tyler was passing by the tent and overheard

his boss wondering where Hathaway was. It looked like it was time to do more damage control.

"Oh, hello, Mr. and Mrs. Drysdale," he said with a smile. "I couldn't help overhearing you wondering about Hathaway. She just called and said that something had come up and you should start the wedding without her."

"What could have come up?" Margaret Drysdale wondered.

"I wish I knew," Tyler said. Eager to get the conversation off Hathaway, he turned to Babette. "My, what a lovely dog."

"Why, thank you." Margaret smiled. Nothing made her happier than when someone complimented her on her prized purebred barbone.

"Look, Tyler," Drysdale said impatiently, "since you're here, you might as well make yourself useful. Go count the olives."

"I'll get on it right away." Tyler dashed off toward the salads.

"God, I hate that little worm," Drysdale muttered under his breath. "And what could Hathaway possibly be doing that's more important than this?"

At that very moment Hathaway, disguised as a nurse and wearing a red wig, was speeding across town toward the Los Viejos Retirement Home. She parked her Miata outside and hurried into the reception area, where she was stopped by a tough-looking orderly.

"Who you here to see?" he asked.

"Oh, uh . . ." Hathaway pretended to thumb through a folder she was carrying. "Daisy May Moses."

"Hmmm." The orderly looked through a ledger on the reception desk. "Oh, yeah. You must be here for the rabies test."

"Yes," Hathaway said. "The rabies test. That's right."

"Well, she's in room five twenty-five," said the orderly. "But you'd better be careful. She's a wild one. They had to give her electroshock therapy."

Hathaway hurried to the elevator and rode up to the fifth floor. She found room 525 and went in.

"Ohmygod!" she couldn't believe what she was seeing. Granny was sitting up in bed, wrapped in a straitjacket. Her eyes were vacant and her hair was frizzed out—clearly from the shock therapy. Hathaway hurried to her side.

"Granny?"

"Inni, minni, minni, inni," Granny mumbled weakly, staring straight in front of her.

Hathaway could see that extraordinary measures were in order. She quickly whipped out Granny's flask and poured some of the "medicine" into her mouth.

Granny swallowed. In a flash her hair went back in place. *Pop! Pop! Pop!* She flexed her arms,

and the straitjacket snapped apart. She turned to Hathaway and blinked.

"Where am I, Miss Hathaway?" she asked.

"You're in a retirement home."

"Me? Heck, I'm too young for this." Granny jumped out of bed. "Let's hightail it out of here!"

As they snuck down the hall Hathaway filled Granny in on the story concerning Miss Laurette. "There's nothing to worry about," she assured her. "I called Tyler and told him to cancel the wedding."

"Tyler!" Granny shouted. "Him and Miss Laurette's the ones that stuck me in this hole to begin with. And she ain't no foreigner."

"God forbid!" Hathaway groaned. "We've been stabbed in the back by one of our own!"

She was just about to say that they'd really have to hurry when Myron Mackey and an orderly appeared at the end of the hall.

"Daisy May Moses wasn't supposed to have her rabies test until tomorrow!" Mackey shouted. "Get them!"

Hathaway and Granny turned and ran. The owner of the retirement home and the orderly raced after them.

Just as they were about to catch them a man in a wheelchair pushed a door open.

Thunk! Mackey and the orderly smashed into it and sank to the ground unconscious.

Hathaway and Granny ran down five flights

of stairs and out to the parking lot, where they jumped in the Miata and sped off for Beverly Hills.

Meanwhile a long caravan of limousines pulled into the Clampett driveway, and nearly a hundred hillbillies poured out of them. Jethro, wearing his best man's tuxedo, came out the front door of the mansion to greet them.

"Ma!" he shouted with joy as Pearl got out of the first limo.

"Jethro, my baby!" Pearl cried, and hugged him. Then she backed up a step and looked him over. "My gracious! Beverly Hills has made you so sophisticated!"

A second later Jethro was blindsided by Jethrine and knocked to the ground.

"Howdy, Jethro!" his twin sister said, and helped him back to his feet. "All this excitement sure has gotten me hungry. I could eat a horse."

Jethro pointed over at the party tent, where waiters dressed in black were carrying trays. "Them fellers over there has got the food, Jethrine. But you've got to stay with 'em because they'll try to keep you from eatin' too much."

"All of you, please be seated," a man in a black tux called, waving from the wedding tent. "The wedding is about to begin."

The hillbillies took their seats together, except for Jethrine, who spotted a handsome

young fellow sitting way in the back with some kind of electronic equipment on his lap.

"Hi there, handsome," she said, sitting down next to him. "Mind if I sit with you?"

Tyler looked up speechless as Jethro's large twin sister sat beside him. Now the Reverend Mason took his place at the altar. He took a pull from his flask and pressed his hands into the small of his back, smiling with relief. The crowd began to hush. Jethro and Jed stepped up to the altar, and the orchestra began the wedding march.

The crowd turned to watch Elly May, in a stunning bridesmaid's dress, start down the aisle. When she saw all her hillbilly kin, she grinned and waved. Spanky, the orangutan, came next, wearing his tuxedo and top hat.

Now Laura started down the aisle in an elegant wedding dress. In the last row Jethrine started to sob and leaned on Tyler's shoulder. Immediately the crowd was abuzz.

In his seat near the altar, Drysdale leaned close to his wife. "Hathaway better have a good excuse for not being here," he whispered.

At the same time Margaret turned and saw that many of the guests' cars were being parked on the Clampett front lawn, among the grazing herd of cattle.

"Look where they're parking the cars!" she whispered in horror. "My God, how tacky!"

Drysdale nodded and stared at the orangutan in the tuxedo. "This is turning into a real zoo," he muttered.

Across the aisle, the hillbillies stared at Miss Laurette.

Pearl leaned toward Spittin' Sam. "Granny told me she don't trust Miss Laurette," she whispered behind her hand.

Spittin' Sam spit angrily and turned to Mayor Jasper. "I think she's tryin' to take Jed for all he's got."

Mayor Jasper turned to Fat Elmer. "I got it in my craw she's up to no good."

"Look at her," Fat Elmer whispered back. "She's so skinny, you couldn't hit her with a handful of corn."

Now Elmer turned to Hank and Frank, who were still wearing their skunk-skin hats. "What do you think about this, boys?"

"It stinks," Hank and Frank whispered back in unison.

As Laurette took her place next to Jed before the altar, Tyler typed on his computer screen:

TRANSFER: $1,000,000,000
FROM: USA BANK # 178-4323 Acct # 054-2324-1254
TO: SWISS BANK # 139-9876-8 Acct # 76-985-4276

Reverend Mason nodded at Jed and Laurette, then took out a Bible. A few business cards and scraps of paper fell out of it as he began to read:

"Dearly beloved, in case of emergency, masks will fall from the overhead compartment. Your seat cushion can be used as a floatation device. Thus sayeth the Lord."

Laurette rolled her eyes and stared skyward in disbelief. Jed leaned toward the reverend.

"Uh, excuse me, Reverend Mason," he said. "I believe you might be reading the wrong passage."

Reverend Mason squinted into the Bible and pulled out an emergency information card from the jet they'd all flown in on that morning.

"Why, I believe you're right, Jed." He cleared his throat and started again. "Dearly beloved, we all are gathered here to unite these two in holy matrimony. . . ."

As the reverend drawled on and on Laura glanced back at Tyler, who winked and gave her the thumbs-up sign. Laura knew it was all going well, but it was taking too darn long.

"Uh, excuse me, Reverend," she whispered.

Reverend Mason looked up, surprised. "Yes?"

"Think you could speed it up a little?"

"Well, I'll try."

Meanwhile Hathaway's Miata raced up to the front gate, where it was stopped by a uniformed security guard.

"Out of the way!" Granny shouted. "We gotta get through."

"Can I see your invitations, ladies?" the guard asked.

"Invitation!" Granny shouted. "I don't need no stinkin' invitation!"

"Excuse me, young man," Hathaway said. "Do you know who you're talking to?"

The guard looked from Granny to Hathaway and back. "Offhand I'd say I'm talking to one crazy lady, and another with a bad wig."

"I ain't wearin' no wig!" Granny exploded. "Every hair on this here head is mine!"

Granny took a swing and tried to sock the guard in the nose, but Hathaway restrained her.

"We'll be back," Hathaway said icily.

Under the tent, the wedding ceremony continued.

"If there be any one of y'all who has one good reason why these two shouldn't be hitched," the Reverend Mason said, "speak now or forever hold your peace."

Laura looked around and smiled. No one uttered a peep. In the back row, Tyler's fingers were poised above the keyboard of his laptop computer, ready to send the message to transfer the funds.

BARROOOMMMMMM! Suddenly there was a loud rumbling sound.

"What in tarnation is that?" Reverend Mason asked. Looking up, he saw the answer.

CRASH! Scattering the security guards, Jethro's monster truck smashed through the front gate, rolled over a couple of cars, and came bouncing and thundering toward the wedding tent.

"Look out!"

"Run!"

Dozens of guests jumped up and ran out of the tent. The truck screeched to a stop, and Hathaway and Granny jumped out.

"Stop the ceremony!" Hathaway shouted.

"Hathaway, have you lost your mind?" Drysdale screamed.

"She's an imposter!" Hathaway cried, pointing at Laura. "She just wants to marry Mr. Clampett for his money!"

"She kidnapped me!" Granny said. Then she pointed at Tyler. "And he helped her!"

Laura picked up the hem of her wedding dress and started to run. Tyler grabbed his computer and took off after her.

"I'm ruined!" Drysdale collapsed on the ground.

If Laura and Tyler thought they could get away, they were mistaken. They suddenly found themselves looking down the twin barrels of a shotgun held by Mayor Jasper.

"Don't leave now, ma'am," the mayor said politely. "The party's just beginning."

Laura and Tyler turned and ran off in another direction, toward the party tent next to the pool.

"Set up the computer!" Laura shouted at Tyler. "If we can't be rich, neither should these hicks. Send their money bouncing to so many banks, they'll never find it."

In the party tent, Tyler swept some food off a

buffet table and put down the computer. His fingers raced over the keyboard:

TRANSFER: **$1,000,000,000**
FROM: USA BANK # 178-4323 ACCT # 054-2324-1254
TO: RANDOM BANKS/*.* ACCT: RANDOM/*.*

As Jed and the others raced toward him Tyler hit the enter button.

"I did it!" he shouted gleefully. "You rustic, nose-pickin', inbred yokels are dirt-poor now!"

Hathaway grabbed the shotgun from Mayor Jasper and aimed it at the computer.

Ker-pow! The little machine exploded into tiny bits. Tyler stared at her and swallowed.

"You know, Miss Hathaway," he said sheepishly. "Some things are said and done in haste . . . things we later come to regret. To tell you the truth, I've always found you to be rather attractive."

"Eat your heart out, baby." Hathaway assumed a karate position and delivered a devastating kick to Tyler's stomach, sending him flying backward into Jethrine's lap.

"Oh, thank the Lord!" Jethrine cried in delight, and kissed him.

Hoping everyone was distracted by Tyler, Laura tried to sneak back toward the driveway, but she ran right into Jed, who just shook his head and looked deeply hurt.

"I just don't understand it, Miss Laurette," he said. "Why would you do such a thing?"

"Because you don't deserve so much money," Laura said spitefully. "I'm the one who should be a billionaire!"

"Believe me, it ain't all it's cracked up to be," Jed said softly.

Someone grabbed Laura from behind. It was Elly May.

"Here's a little etiquette I'd like to teach you," she yelled, swinging Laura over her head and hurling her into a buffet table with a crash.

Jethro ran up. "Uncle Jed, does this mean we ain't havin' the weddin'?"

"I'm afraid not," Jed replied sadly. Then he brightened slightly. "I guess we're gonna skip the hitchin' and get right to the shindig. Weeeee-doggies!"

He grabbed his shotgun from Mayor Jasper, aimed it in the air, and fired.

"Yahhh-hooo!" All the hillbillies hooted and hollered and started firing their guns. A cousin named Billy Bob and some other hillbillies got up where the orchestra had been and started playin' hootenanny music.

Hank and Frank grabbed Laura and dragged her into the dancing crowd, where they made sure she got spun and thrown around until she could hardly stand. Meanwhile Jethrine had Tyler in a bear hug as she danced around the floor.

In the midst of it all, Jed sat off by himself, watching the festivities. Elly May came over and sat with him.

"Aw, Pa," she said, taking his hand. "You must be so disappointed."

"A little," Jed admitted. "But I was mainly marryin' Miss Laurette 'cause I thought you wanted her for your ma."

Elly May squeezed his hand. "I'm so sorry, Pa. If I wasn't so wild, you wouldn't need no new ma for me."

"Now, don't be sorry," Jed said. "I love the way you are. And I reckon I should raise you to be who you want to be. I know that's what your ma would have wanted."

"I don't need a new ma," Elly May said. "Not as long as I have you and Granny."

They were interrupted by a group of policemen, who stepped onto the dance floor. Hank and Frank let go of Laura, and Jethrine let go of Tyler. The two accomplices collapsed on the floor.

"You're under arrest for kidnapping, attempted embezzlement, and fraud," the police sergeant announced. Laura and Tyler were handcuffed and led away.

"Git these low-life varmints off our property!" Granny shouted, shaking her fist.

"I admit it freely," Tyler sobbed, pointing at Laura. "It was all her idea."

Jethrine waved a lace hanky at him. "I'll wait for you, honey!" she cried. Then she shook her head and sniffed. "I always fall for the wrong kind of man."

The music started up again, and Jethro stepped up to Hathaway. "Hot dog, Miss Jane," he said. "You sure are a good shot."

Hathaway grabbed Granny's flask and took a big gulp. Then she grabbed Jethro and twirled him onto the dance floor. Not far away, in the bushes at the edge of the dance floor, Morgan and his mother searched for Babette.

"It's not like her to run away like this," Margaret said. "Babette! Come to Mama, sweetie!"

"Where are you, you overpriced ball of fur?" Morgan muttered.

Woof! They heard a bark. Morgan parted a bush and found Babette and Duke presiding over a dozen half-poodle, half-hound mutts.

"Ohmygod!" Margaret fainted dead away on the grass.

"Hey, everyone!" Morgan shouted. "Come look!"

Jed, Granny, and Elly May went to see the puppies. Drysdale followed.

"I'm terribly sorry about what happened," the bank president said apologetically. "I hope you don't think everyone in Beverly Hills is like those money-grubbing city slickers. We all want you to stay."

"Well, that's up to Elly May," Jed said. "What do you think, darlin'?"

"Heck, I'm captain of the rasslin' team, Pa," Elly May said. "We gotta stay. That is, if it's all right with you."

"I reckon I can git used to this place," Jed said. "So I guess that means we're stayin'."

"Well, then, we'd better commence to findin' Elly May a husband," Granny said. "She's almost seventeen. Folks'll soon be callin' her an old maid!"

"We can wait till tomorrow to do that," Jed said merrily. "Right now I suggest we keep on partyin'."

Once again he raised his shotgun to the sky and fired. Then everyone joined in the fun.

EPILOGUE

The pellets from Jed's shotgun flew high into the sky, then hurled back toward earth, kicking up a small chunk of earth in a far corner of the Clampett estate.

For a moment the earth was still.

Then a thick, gooey black substance began to bubble up through the ground.

Some people call it Texas tea. . . . Oil, that is.

TODD STRASSER has written many award-winning novels for both adults and teenagers. Several of his works have been adapted for the screen, including *Workin' for Peanuts, A Very Touchy Subject,* and *Over the Limit,* which he adapted himself. A former newspaper reporter and advertising copywriter, Strasser worked for several years as a television scriptwriter on such shows as "The Guiding Light," "Tribes," and "Riviera." The author of nearly forty novels, Strasser lives with his family in a suburb of New York City.